Martha's Mirror

JESS WIMMER

Dedicated to Grammy
for all of the nights we spent watching Ghost Adventures.

Chapter 1

I re-read the text. "Zoey, we're so excited for you to join us for the annual Halloween party at the historic Meridion Manor. Your assigned costume for the night is Mrs. Meridion. Please dress accordingly and prepare to play the part. Historical information regarding your character is on our website."

I scanned through the countless outfits flung across the carpet and looked back at the open closet. Laying back against my grey and black paisley duvet, I groaned.

Dress accordingly. What does that even mean?

A huff of air escaped my lips as I lifted my head slightly so that I could see my phone screen. I clicked the link and selected the photo gallery icon. I scrolled past photos of the manor's summer fling, the Valentine's Day ball and the winter feast before finally coming to photos from last year's Halloween party. A group photo from the event showed men dressed in suits that I imagined the ringleader of a haunted circus would wear. The women wore floor length gowns with full bustle skirts and fitted bodices with long sleeves puffed at the shoulder. It looked just like something my mother would have sewn. *You have got to be kidding me.* I let my head fall back against the bed.

I loved everything that went along with Halloween; the haunted houses, the movies, the music, but I hated dressing up.

Throughout my childhood, my mother crafted budget-friendly costumes out of whatever fabric or old clothes we had lying around. She was a single mom working as a late-night gas station attendant, so it was hard to blame her for our lack of funds. It's not like she asked my father to abandon her before I was born. She really tried hard, but I just couldn't take the embarrassment anymore.

After the Halloween costume contest in sixth grade, when my mother insisted I enter her handmade superhero-inspired monstrosity, I had to save myself from further humiliation. The following year I swore to her that I was just too old for costumes and begged her to let me watch a horror movie for the first time instead. From that day forward, she would take the night off of work every

Halloween, and we would watch a marathon of horror movies together.

Unfortunately, our tradition didn't even last a decade. During the spring semester of my junior year in college, she hit a deer on the way home from work. I never even got the chance to say goodbye.

The loss devastated me. I couldn't bear to watch the movies without her, and I couldn't stomach the thought of allowing someone else to take her place. During the last two Halloweens, instead of watching horror movies, I spent the night people watching with my next-door neighbor and old friend, Carter.

We positioned ourselves in folding chairs on the patio of our shared building and turned the porch lights off so that no one would come to the door. Then we spent the night observing the drunken shenanigans of the local college crowd. We even made a drinking game of it, taking a sip each time we watched someone trip on the uneven sidewalk just beyond the gravel parking lot. This year, however, our drinking game will be on hold until later in the night.

My friend Cameron, who worked at a bar downtown with me, had guilted me into attending a party with him at the Meridion manor. When he invited me, he explained that the manor was a Victorian era estate that had been home to a wealthy business mogul and his family. Many visitors, according to Cameron at least, had reported hearing noises and being touched by unseen forces. Like me, Cameron loved the darker side of life. Specifically, he loved trying to convince people that ghosts really exist and I was one of the few people that entertained his theories about the paranormal. I gave into his begging when he assured me there would be no horror movies involved in the party. However, he had neglected to mention that it was a role-playing party and that costumes are required. I decided a little bit of teasing was warranted, so I texted him.

Zoey: Thanks for the heads up about the costumes. Am I supposed to know who Mrs. Meridion is?

Cameron: You wouldn't have agreed to come if I told you LOL. How do you not know who she is? She's like the most important character besides Mr. Meridion.

Zoey: Great, thanks. Totally clears things up.

Cameron: OMG, didn't you pay attention in history class! She's the wife of Landon Meridion. They owned the manor in the 1800s.

Zoey: Can't I just dress up as a ghost or something?

Cameron: Technically, Mrs. Meridion is a ghost. She died like 200 years ago.

I sighed as I rose from the bed and sifted through my clothes once more, channeling my mother's costume creativity.

There has to be something here I can make work.

I finally gave up searching for proper attire. With only a few hours to prepare for the party and no car to get me there, I had no choice but to ask my neighbor for a ride to the store. I exited my apartment and knocked on the only other door in the small two-unit brick building. Carter, whom I'd reconnected with since living in the apartment, quickly opened the door to reveal beads of sweat trickling down his bare torso.

"Hey, Zoey," he said, out of breath, as he wiped a towel across his forehead. "What's up?"

"Sorry, I didn't mean to interrupt your workout," I mumbled, trying not to stare.

He shrugged. "I was basically done anyways. What do you need?"

I bit my upper lip. Asking him for help always made me feel guilty, especially since I knew it would give him the wrong idea about my feelings for him. He'd been trying to get me to go on a date with him for months. I silently cursed Cameron for taking the afternoon shift in lieu of the late shift tonight, I'd feel a lot better asking him to drive me.

"Umm, do you think...I mean, if you're not too busy...could you, maybe, drive me to the store?" I asked.

Carter laughed. "Of course."

I nodded. "Okay, but, umm...as long as it's not going to..."

He cut me off, "Zo, it's no big deal. I've told you a thousand times, I'm happy to give you a ride anytime."

"Thanks," I mumbled, my eyes aimed at the concrete porch.

He looked at his bare chest, and I hoped he didn't notice me following his gaze.

"Let me just grab a shirt, then we can go," he said.

I nodded and retreated to my apartment, selecting a sweatshirt from the floor. Pulling it over my arms, I zipped it halfway as I returned to the porch where Carter was waiting in a V-neck t-shirt that hugged his biceps. I followed him to his sedan and sat in the passenger seat. He turned the key and looked at me with a grin. The color in his eyes sparkled against the blue in his shirt as he asked, "Where to?"

I exhaled. "The Halloween store."

He raised an eyebrow at me, seemingly amused. "Zoey Martin, as in Batgirl, wants to go to the Halloween store?"

I sighed at the reminder of my last Halloween costume and with an eye roll, I explained my predicament.

"Cameron insisted on going to this party at Meridion manor. He conveniently didn't tell me that costumes were required until I'd already promised to go. I can't find anything to wear, so I'm hoping the Halloween store has something that will work."

"My apartment is always available for hiding purposes, if you don't want to go." He winked in an attempt to entice me as he put the car in drive. I hated to admit it, but it almost worked.

Sometimes I wished we hadn't known each other prior to moving into this building. I always wondered if I might see him differently if I didn't know who he was back then.

Carter and I were friends in elementary school, but once he joined the high school football team, being seen with 'the girl in rags,' as they called me, was equivalent to calling yourself a loser.

He did his best to avoid me in high school, but it didn't take long for the rest of his team to realize how well we knew each other. After that, he went out of his way to distance himself from me.

Senior year, he even stood by and watched as the captain of the football team, who'd gotten ahold of the PA system, announced to the entire school that he and the rest of the team had collectively decided they wouldn't date me if I was the last girl alive.

It had taken a lot for me to forgive him for that. Cameron still held it against him and often encouraged me not to trust him, but it was hard to hold a grudge after everything he'd done for me recently.

I glared at him. "I promised him I would go. " I added, "you know me, I don't back out if I commit to something."

He shrugged, keeping his eyes on the road. "He's just some loser from work. Who cares?"

"I can't just ditch him, Carter," I spat. "Plus, he's not just some guy from work. He's my best friend."

"If I were you, I would ditch him," he mumbled, "you're so out of his league."

I huffed. "How many times do I have to tell you? My relationship with Cameron is not like that."

"He certainly comes over to your apartment a lot for someone you're not into," he grumbled.

I shook my head. "You're unbelievable."

"I'm just saying you could do better," he said.

I turned my body to face him, trying to ensure that my annoyance was evident in my expression. "And what would be better? Going to the party with the guy who laughed me off of the stage last time I wore a costume?"

I'd never forget the betrayal I felt as I moped across the stage in shame, the worn elastic of mom's old black swimsuit sagging three inches below the faded, torn jeans

I'd been wearing for years. Sometimes it still made me want to cry, thinking about the way he and his friends had snickered at the piece of notebook paper featuring a hand drawn bat that was safety-pinned to my breasts.

"How many times do I have to apologize for that?" he asked, reaching for my hand.

"One more time couldn't hurt," I replied with a teasing smile.

"I'm sorry I laughed at you," he said, "Hana's costume was far inferior to yours."

"Thank you," I sassed before scowling at the thought of her.

Hana Brodwik was the head cheerleader he'd hooked up with a few times in high school. I wanted nothing more than to punch her as she strutted past me that day in a sleek black gymnastics outfit that clung to her in all of the right places. The thought of the professionally bedazzled gold bat on her chest made me want to puke.

"I hope she gets bit by a bat," I snorted, and he laughed.

"I bet you'd make a really hot Batgirl nowadays," he slyly replied, and I raised an eyebrow, skeptically.

"What do you say?" he asked. "I'll be Batman, and we can just hang out in my apartment. You and I, Batman and Batgirl."

I scoffed. Carter had been desperately vying for my attention since I moved in. He claimed he wanted to make up for the way he acted in high school. But, unfortunately for him, I wasn't interested in a romantic relationship with him, or anyone, for that matter. He was nice enough and made me laugh, but every time I went to his apartment, the letterman jacket on his coat rack haunted me.

I sighed. "Carter, we've talked about this. I don't really want a relationship with anyone right now."

"Why don't you invite Hana over?" I suggested.

"I haven't talked to her in years," Carter replied, "and I know you're not looking, but you can't blame me for trying to change your mind, can you?"

I rolled my eyes. "Good luck with that."

Carter stopped in a parking space outside the outlets, and we walked together into the Halloween store.

He immediately picked up a bunny costume that looked more like a swimsuit to me. Gleaming, he said, "I think this one is perfect."

I scowled at him. "Keep dreaming."

"You're no fun," he laughed, returning the package to its hanger.

I quickly scanned the aisles for anything that resembled what I'd seen on the website while Carter tried on masks in the back of the store. I came upon a costume titled

"Pioneer Woman" and thought, *that'll have to work.* Eager to leave the store, I rushed through the main aisle in search of Carter and discovered him in the midst of a pirate sword duel with a young boy.

"How old are you?" I teased as Carter fell to the floor in defeat, to the delight of the boy.

He looked at his young foe and whispered loudly. "She's not cool enough to sword fight."

The boy laughed as Carter stood. Carter pointed to the package in my hand. "What did you find?"

I begrudgingly lifted my hand so that he could see.

"Interesting choice," he said, raising an eyebrow.

"I have to dress as Mrs. Meridion," I explained, making air quotes with my hands as I said the name.

"Is that like Cameron's mom or something?" Carter laughed.

I playfully hit him with the costume bag, "no," I laughed. "She was the wife of the man who owned the manor."

"I know who Mrs. Meridion is," he said, pretending to be insulted. He leaned in to whisper, "you know, legend has it Mr. Meridion hid his brother's body inside the manor."

"Oh, yeah?" I encouraged him.

"Yeah, supposedly he still haunts the manor," he wrapped his arms around my waist from behind and spoke into my ear. "You might need me to hold your hand..." He paused before playfully tickling my torso, "when the ghost gets you."

I ignored his teasing, he knew I didn't scare easily. But my mood brightened at the thought of having someone else I knew at the party. I casually wiggled out of his grasp.

"Are you going to be there tonight?" I asked, maybe a little too eagerly.

"I didn't buy tickets," he said, "but I would if you really wanted me to."

I shrugged teasingly as we approached the checkout counter. "Too bad it's sold out."

He smiled and placed his hand on my shoulder. "The offer still stands to hide at my place."

"If I change my mind, you'll be the first to know." I assured him, taking my receipt from the cashier.

***

When we returned to the apartment building, Carter gave me one last chance to bail on the party before returning to his apartment. I listened for the familiar sound of Carter's weight set being moved and nodded to myself, satisfied that he'd found a distraction. Then, I noticed a text from Cameron.

Cameron: Be there in 10.

Zoey: Sounds good.

I hurriedly removed the costume from its package and put it on, groaning as I inspected myself in the mirror. The tan plaid dress puffed out in all the wrong places and the white lining around the buttons reminded me of Laura Ingalls. *I look ridiculous.*

As I finished braiding my hair, I heard a car door close, followed by a knock at my door. Wrapping a hair tie around the end of my auburn braid, I made my way to the front door and opened it. Cameron stood in white pants and a white button-down shirt. His costume was complete with a chef's hat atop his curly red hair.

"Sexy, right?" He joked, spinning on the porch so I could see all angles of his costume. He ended the spin with a flamboyant pose.

"Not as sexy as me," I joked, curtsying.

Carter's door opened just as Cameron pinched the fabric on my upper arm. "You're definitely getting all the guys tonight, Mrs. Meridion," Cameron teased.

"Get a room." Carter snorted, taking a sip from the beer bottle in his hand as he leaned his bare back against the front of the building.

"Knock it off, Carter." I tilted my head in a plea.

Cameron rolled his eyes, refusing to look at Carter, then smiled at me. "Ready to go?"

"Yep," I chimed, waving goodbye to Carter as I approached the passenger side of Cameron's car. Carter lifted his beer and yelled, "don't forget my offer, Zo."

I smiled at him and nodded in acknowledgement as I got into the car.

"He's such a douche." Cameron muttered as he drove us to the manor.

I exhaled. "He's not that bad."

"He convinced half the school you were asexual, so that they wouldn't think he liked you," Cameron reminded me.

"He's more mature now," I replied.

"Since when," Cameron snorted.

"Ever since my mom died," I replied. "It's like he thinks he can take away the pain of her death by making amends or something."

"How many times has he asked you out this week?" Cameron wondered out loud, lightening the mood, his eyes on the road.

"Twice." I giggled.

"And I thought I was desperate," Cameron said, turning the steering wheel.

"Here we are," he beamed as he parked the car.

I took in the breathtaking three-story building constructed of mahogany planks with sapphire trim. Black steel banisters lined the wrap-around porch and the dark tinted windows of the second and third floors added a touch of mystery to the manor. The sunlight beginning to fade over the orchard surrounding the building reminded me of the many movies I'd watched with my mother. An eerie feeling set in as I tried not to think about who or what could be lurking amongst the trees.

"This place looks straight out of a horror movie," I commented.

We stepped onto the porch, and the planks let out a spooky creak. Cameron stopped and turned to me with an evil grin. "Nothing says haunted mansion like creaky floorboards."

Seeing me gulp down the slight fear he'd instilled, he bounced up and down on the planks, causing a chorus of squeaking noises.

"Knock it off," I laughed.

He opened the door of the manor and gestured for me to enter. "Ladies first."

***

An older woman in a Victorian dress identical in color to the siding of the building greeted us in the lobby. She wore black ribbon accents around her waist and a matching sunhat sat atop her head.

"Gather in the lobby please. We'll get started shortly," she announced, gesturing to the surrounding room. As we waited for the woman to give further instructions, Cameron swayed to the ballroom music playing softly throughout the room. I shook my head as I giggled and looked around to see if he was drawing attention to us. I noticed a tall man dressed as a ringleader with short, dark hair peeking under his top hat. His brown eyes reflected the light of the extravagant chandelier above as he approached us.

Cameron stopped dancing and almost yelled at the man, "Nolan!"

"Hey, man, looking good," the man greeted Cameron, looking him up and down.

Becoming aware of my discomfort, Cameron wrapped his arm around my shoulder. "This is Zoey. She works at the bar with me."

The man raised his hand in a wave. "I'm Nolan...Cameron's friend."

"Nice to meet you," I smiled shyly, looking at Cameron. "New boyfriend?" I asked him.

Nolan laughed. "No, I'm straight."

Cameron winked at him. "For now."

He looked Nolan up and down, pointing to his outfit. "Who are you supposed to be?"

He raised his hands, gesturing to his coat as if it was obvious. "Mr. Meridion."

Cameron's face lit up as he looked from me to Nolan. "No way! Zoey is Mrs. Meridion!"

He leaned forward and held a hand up to block my view of his mouth as he loudly whispered, "she's single."

I tried to look to the floor, but Nolan's eyes met mine.

"Thanks for the heads up," Nolan replied.

The woman who'd greeted us clapped three times, and Cameron stepped forward to listen intently, leaving Nolan and I standing next to each other.

Nolan leaned toward me and whispered, "So, I guess he conned you into this, too?"

I slowly turned to him, grabbing the skirt of my dress. "Yeah. I hate costume parties."

He giggled, a little too loudly. "Me, too."

The woman who'd clapped glared at us and we sucked our mouths shut.

She continued her speech, "hello everyone and welcome to Meridion Manor. I am Ellie Fadra, the president of the historical society. We're so pleased to host this party for the twelfth year in a row. I want you all to have as much time as possible to explore the history of this wonderful estate," she explained. "So, very quickly, could Mr. and Mrs. Meridion, and Martha, please step forward."

Nolan and I looked at each other and took a step toward her. She smiled.

"Very good. The two of you are husband and wife, so I expect to see you together throughout the night. You'll start in the peach room. Remember, accents make it more fun, the Meridion's would have had trans-Atlantic accents."

She turned to the slightly younger girl across from us and continued. "And you, Martha. The Meridion's daughter spent a lot of time in her room. I would recommend getting acquainted with it. It's on the third floor, second door on the right."

She spun to address the rest of the group. "Now, everyone else. Chefs, I expect you know where the kitchen is located. Butlers, you each received a station through text. Dinner guests will begin in the dining room, etc. etc."

She clapped once more. "Have fun, drinks are in the kitchen, I hope you learn something, and of course, any questions find me."

"I have a question," a boy, dressed as a farmhand, said from the other side of the room.

"Yes?" Ms. Fadra replied.

"Is this place really haunted?" he asked.

She giggled to herself, and I guessed that she wasn't a believer. "Maybe if you're lucky the Meridion's will say hello tonight," she offered.

The girl playing Martha leaned over to me and whispered, "I can feel a presence here."

I looked at her like she was insane and chose not to respond.

"Enjoy married life," Cameron said with a wink before skipping toward the kitchen.

As partygoers disbursed around the manor, Nolan and I looked to each other for direction. Finally, I addressed him. "Any idea where the peach room is?"

He lifted his hands and shrugged. "No clue, but I think the kitchen is over there," he said pointing to my left.

I nodded. "Right, drinks. Good idea."

Nolan headed straight for a bottle of Cabernet and poured himself a glass before lifting the bottle toward me. "Are you a wine girl or a beer girl?"

I pointed at the bottle in his hand. "Wine."

"Nice!" He nodded in approval before filling a second glass and handing it to me. He continued, "not to brag, but I'm a bit of a connoisseur."

"Oh yeah? What's your favorite?" I asked.

"I'm usually a chardonnay guy, but I'll settle for red," he said, raising his glass to his lips.

"I like chardonnay too," I replied, taking a sip of the red wine he'd handed me.

"Should we go find the peach room?" he suggested.

I nodded as I took a sip from my glass and followed Nolan to the staircase in the lobby.

"I'm going to guess it's upstairs," he said as I trailed behind him.

As we reached the second floor and began wandering the hallway, I inquired about his relationship with my friend. "So how do you know Cameron?"

He kept walking as he casually explained, "we were roommates all four years of college."

"So, I guess you guys still hang out quite a bit?" I inferred, following him down the hall.

A light bulb flickered in a sconce on the wall, causing him to stop. He looked at the light and shrugged it off, turning his head toward the open door beside him.

"Yeah, we do pizza and a movie pretty much every Friday," he replied.

As I took the last few steps to meet him at the doorway, I commented, "I would definitely choose pizza over this. I can't believe he convinced me to wear this outfit."

He laughed, looking from his outfit to mine. "Like you said, Cameron can be quite convincing."

"Cheers to that," I said, raising my glass. He clinked his against it and we drank before inspecting the room.

"This room looks pretty peachy to me," he said, placing a hand on a wall, which was papered in peach and cream stripes accented by dark walnut chair rail molding and a pristine cream carpet. A handmade rocking chair sat in the back corner next to a tinted window, and an armoire stood in the opposite corner. A large four-poster bed sat against the wall to the left of the doorway, covered in a duvet that matched the wallpaper. On the wall across from the bed hung an oil painting of a couple who appeared slightly older than the two of us.

"Do you think that's Mr. and Mrs. Meridion?" I wondered, casually sipping my wine.

He inspected the portrait. "If it is, I did a pretty dang good job with my outfit."

I looked at his maroon suit. It was nearly identical to the one in the painting. I agreed as goose bumps formed on my forearms. Crossing my arms to combat the chill, I looked at Nolan, who shook ever so slightly before looking toward the window.

"For such an expensive house, you'd think they'd seal the windows," he said.

"Yeah, really," I agreed. "I think I saw a fireplace somewhere."

He nodded. "I think I saw one across from the lobby downstairs. Do you want to go warm up and then see if we can find Cam?"

"Sounds good to me," I agreed, following him out of the room.

He stopped in the hallway and placed his hand on his stomach, creating a nook in his elbow for my arm to rest.

"I forgot. We're supposed to be married."

I linked my arm with his. "What a gentleman you are, dear," I said in my best trans-Atlantic accent.

He responded in a similarly unconvincing accent, "Might I interest you in another glass of wine, darling?"

"Why yes, you might," I replied as he led me down the hallway.

Stopping at the top of the stairs, Nolan dropped his arm and held up a hand, my palm resting against his.

"Allow me to escort you to the kitchen, my dear," he said.

I placed my other hand over my lips. "Why, thank you. You are a mighty fine gentleman."

We descended the staircase giggling, the alcohol starting to relax our nerves.

As we reached the bottom of the spiral staircase, Cameron came into view, his white shirt already sporting a purple wine stain.

He slurred, "Hey, guys!"

"This is why you're not allowed to wear white," I said, shaking my head and gesturing toward the mess on his shirt.

He looked at his shirt, and then lazily placed his arm over Nolan's shoulder. He pointed to the stain with his other hand. "Turns out Martha isn't a huge fan of the chef's choice," he slurred.

Nolan and I eyed each other. We both knew that Cameron was referring to his signature sexual innuendo.

Nolan groaned. "Dude, tell me you didn't offer her the Cameron special?"

He nodded cockily at Nolan, and I shook my head as I scolded him, "this is why you're single."

Cameron drunkenly draped his left arm over my shoulder, keeping his right on Nolan's. "You guys are single too," he said, pulling us together so that our cheeks touched his.

Nolan placed his hand behind Cameron's back to prevent him from falling over.

"And you're drunk," Nolan said, steadying him.

"Better hope Carter doesn't find out you got married without his permission," Cameron joked, stumbling backward into another room.

I shook my head, changing the subject as I pointed to the room Cameron had stumbled into. "There's the fire, let's warm up."

Nolan moved his arm to my lower back as we walked into the warm room and stopped to stand in front of the flames. Above the stone mantel hung a portrait of a family that I presumed were the Meridions. A woman with soft eyes and dark hair pulled tightly into a bun at the back of her head stood to the right. The man on her left had black hair and stood proudly beside his wife in a black vest and dress pants, his mustache perfectly groomed. And the daughter, Martha, with black hair and freckles symmetrically placed across both cheeks, stared emotionlessly back at us.

"Martha was really pretty," I commented, and Nolan agreed.

"She looks like you," he said casually, and then added, "if you had black hair."

I smiled into my glass, pretending to take a sip as I heard a whisper close to my ear. I turned to him. "What?"

"Oh, I was just..." he stumbled over his words, "I was just saying she kind of looks like you."

"No, I heard that." I replied, turning to see if someone else was with us, but Cameron had disappeared.

"I thought you said something after that," I clarified.

He shook his head.

"Huh," I said, "I must be hearing things."

"We're not even an hour in. Don't go crazy on me," he teased.

A chair fell over next to me, causing one of the butler characters to trip, spilling a glass of champagne on me.

In horror, he rushed to dry my dress with a white cloth, and I waved him away. "It's no big deal. I hate this dress anyway," I assured him.

"I'm so sorry," he insisted, "I don't know what happened."

"That chair moved all by itself," the girl playing Martha stated plainly from the entryway. We spun to look at her as she continued her ominous speech, "I told Miss Fadra it was a bad idea to mock the Meridions with these costumes. They're coming for us."

Her eyes wide, she backed out of the room and then turned and walked away.

"No more wine for her," Nolan whispered jokingly.

"Better watch out, Mr. Meridion is going to get you," I nudged him.

He rolled his eyes. "You sound like Cameron."

"You don't believe in ghosts?" I inquired.

"No, you live, you die, people move on," he shrugged, eyeing me for a response.

"I guess I kind of agree," I shrugged. "If ghosts existed, my mom would have contacted me by now," I nonchalantly added.

He thought for a moment and offered, "mine died too. About five years ago."

"Sorry," I mumbled.

He shrugged.

I awkwardly sipped my drink, unsure of how to change the topic.

"I don't believe in ghosts," he said again. Then offered, "but maybe there's some truth to the tales about the Appalachian Mountains."

"Yeah? Like what?" I asked.

"I've always been terrified of skin walkers," he admitted, and I shivered at the thought of them.

"Yeah, they creep me out too," I said, anxiously peeking out the window. "But ghosts are just as creepy," I added.

"Let's go see what else this manor has to offer," Nolan suggested, changing the subject.

I nodded, following him back toward the staircase. This time paying more attention to the eerie way the wood creaked with each step up. *Could there be ghosts here?* I couldn't help but wonder.

We wandered through the countless rooms of the manor observing the intricate interior design, such as the ornate corner pieces that complimented the crown molding.

As we explored the third floor, we came to a large mint colored room with mahogany floors and an elegant gold chandelier.

Across from the luxurious bed hung an ornate oval shaped mirror. We approached the mirror and Nolan stood slightly behind me as we looked into it. He stuck his tongue out playfully and I laughed, making a face back at his reflection.

I noticed a plaque on the wall near the bottom left of the mirror and moved to read it:

"This mirror was given to Martha Meridion by her uncle, Reginald Bauer, on her 21st birthday. Just a week later, on February 14, 1908, Martha Meridion died of tuberculosis in her bedroom."

"Wow, Martha died at twenty-one," I commented, "that's so young."

A cool air settled across the room as I spoke, and I pulled my arms to my chest for warmth.

"It was pretty common for people to die young back then," Nolan said, sipping his drink. "She's actually lucky to have lived that long with the way TB spread in this area."

I raised an eyebrow at him. "Are you like a walking encyclopedia or something?"

He shrugged, "I'm a teacher."

My expression softened, "oh, that's really cool."

He nodded. "What do you do?"

"I'm a bartender at O'Connell's," I said, adding, "me and Cameron usually work the same shift."

"I thought you looked familiar," he said. "Cam and I hang out there after his shift all the time."

Realization flooded over my face. "Are you the guy that sang "Margaritaville" with Cameron last weekend?"

He laughed nervously, looking at the carpet. "Yeah, not my proudest moment."

"I've heard worse." I shrugged.

He laughed. "I highly doubt that."

Interrupting the moment, the mirror's reflective surface caught my attention.

"Did you see that?" I asked.

"It was probably just a bug," Nolan reasoned.

Confused, I replayed what I'd just seen in my mind. A small cream light had just flickered in the mirror, and then glided out of view, right in front of me. I shook my head. "It didn't move like a bug."

"What else would it be?" He whispered, allowing his fingers to brush against the fabric of my dress. "A ghost?" he teased.

I playfully pushed his hand away.

He slowly slid his hands around my waist, inviting me to step toward him. I rested my hands on his biceps as I did and allowed my eyes to trail from his chest to his lips, and then to his chocolate eyes. Sucking my lips in shyly, I tried to look away, but he moved his right hand to the side of my face and hesitated, as if asking for permission to lean in.

The floor creaked outside the door to the room, jolting us out of the moment. Embarrassingly, I clung to Nolan in fear, before realizing who had joined us.

"If I knew I'd be interrupting something, I wouldn't have come looking for you two," Cameron slurred.

I reluctantly lowered my hands and stepped away from Nolan.

"I was going to ask if you guys wanted another drink," he winked. "But maybe I should close the door for you instead?"

"Shut up," I teased, grabbing a pillow from the bed and playfully throwing it at him.

We followed Cameron to the stairs and gasped in unison as he tripped off the second to last step and collapsed forward, his hands clapping against the tile. As Nolan helped him to his feet, I slipped Cameron's car keys from the pocket of his pants. He vomited across the floor.

"Okay, let's get you home," Nolan said, Cameron leaning into his shoulder.

I helped Nolan guide Cameron to the parking lot, and a fire truck passed by on the road, its sirens blaring. Suddenly, Cameron shoved away from Nolan and took off across the parking lot. I stood, stunned, as Nolan raced to catch him.

Following close behind, I held up my skirt as we approached the field. Nolan pounced on Cameron, tackling him to the ground, and as I got closer, Nolan held him, rocking back and forth as if soothing a child.

He whispered to Cameron, "it's okay, we're all okay."

"What the hell is going on?" I said, still stunned by my friend's odd behavior.

Cameron stood without speaking and looked down at his shirt, which was now green and purple from the grass and the wine.

Nolan replied for him, in a whisper, "he went through a lot as a kid."

It wasn't much of an explanation, but they clearly weren't interested in discussing it further tonight. I elected to let it go for now.

"I'll drive Cameron home," I said.

I unlocked the door to Cameron's car and watched as Nolan helped him into the passenger seat.

"Get home safe," Nolan said as I started the car.

"You too," I said, waving at him as I closed the car door.

Chapter 2

I returned home from work after yet another shift that didn't end in Nolan singing karaoke with Cam. Maybe it was time to give up and move on.

I set my bags on a kitchen bar stool and moved to the cabinets in search of a desperately needed meal. I collected pasta, tomato sauce and spices and retrieved a pot to start dinner. Selecting a playlist on my phone, I danced with a glass of wine while I waited for the water to boil. I lifted a spaghetti spoon from a drawer with my right hand and stirred the pasta into the pot. As I laid the utensil on the counter, an uneasy feeling came over me, as if I was being watched. I hit pause on my phone and slowed my breathing so I could listen for movement, afraid someone might be in the apartment with me. A muted tapping from another room caused me to peek over my shoulder toward the hallway. I waited a moment and heard yet another tap at the wall. The sounds of Carter's weightlifting echoed through the building seconds later and I returned my focus to the pasta, satisfied that he had caused the tapping sound.

My head jerked right as the tap-tap sounded once more, this time clearly from the bathroom. I set down the spoon and slid a butcher knife out of the block on the counter. Weapon in hand, I made my way to where the kitchen tile met the carpet of the hallway and peaked around the wall toward the bathroom. My breath as shaky as my hands, I carefully stepped toward the partially opened bathroom door, my back pinned against the wall and the knife protectively in front of me. I side-stepped quickly past the doorway and took off through the front door, not bothering to close it behind me.

I rushed to the apartment next door and pounded at it like an ape, periodically checking to make sure no one had followed me.

Carter raised an eyebrow at the knife in my hand when he opened the door. He hesitantly asked, "Hey, Zo, what's up?"

I cautiously looked over my shoulder at the wide-open door to my apartment and whispered, "Carter, there's someone in my bathroom."

He looked concerned. Grabbing a baseball bat from behind his front door, he pushed past me onto the patio and approached my door.

"Stay here," he instructed as he entered the apartment wielding the bat.

I couldn't help but admit to myself, the way he was defending me, shirtless no less, was kind of hot.

I peaked over his shoulder as he entered my unit, making his way down the hall toward the bathroom, bat at the ready. Watching from the porch, I held my breath as he freed a hand from the bat just long enough to throw the bathroom door open. His muscles relaxed, and he allowed the bat to fall to his side.

"There's nothing here, Zo," he announced, with a sigh of relief.

"Are you sure?" I hesitantly stepped through the doorway and asked down the hall as he quickly surveyed the remainder of the apartment.

Carter met me at the front door and confirmed, "definitely no one here."

I took a deep breath and explained my behavior, "I swear I heard something tapping on the mirror."

He shrugged. "You're probably just stressed. You always get this way in the fall," he reminded me.

I nodded slowly, refusing to take my eyes off the bathroom. "You're right," I finally agreed, "thanks for checking."

"Anytime," he replied with a smile.

As he stepped on the patio to leave, he turned around and offered, "I have a bottle of whiskey if you want to take the edge off."

Normally I wouldn't take Carter up on anything that might indicate I was accepting his advances, but I was desperate not to be alone with whatever was causing the tapping.

"Okay," I agreed.

Carter returned to his apartment triumphantly and retrieved the aforementioned bottle. While I waited for him to return, I finished the pasta, then cautiously opened the bathroom door to verify that the room was, in fact, empty. Satisfied that Carter had been right, I began to pull the door shut, flinging it back open as a single tap sounded from the area around the sink.

I frantically scanned the countertop for the source of the sound, finding nothing other than a bottle of mascara that had fallen on its side. I closed my eyes and silently laughed at myself for being scared by such a trivial sound, but when my eyes reopened, I wondered, *how did this fall over so many times?*

I pinched the small bottle between my thumb and index finger and lightly tapped it against the mirror and threw the bottle at the counter in terror. That was indeed the noise I'd heard, *but how?*

Mustering all the courage I had, I leaned toward the mirror to inspect it. My heavy breathing formed a cloud of fog against the glass, and I gasped as faint words appeared on the mirror from the warmth of my breath. Instinctively, I blew another breath of hot air against the mirror, revealing a message, "he'll come for you."

I screamed and Carter barreled through the front door, depositing two shot glasses and a bottle of whiskey on the half wall before barging into the bathroom.

"What's wrong?" he asked, out of breath.

I pointed to the mirror, pressing myself into his chest out of fear.

He held me for a moment, then leaned back to look down at me. "What's wrong?" he asked again.

"The mirror," I said, pointing to where the message had been.

"There's nothing there, Zo," he assured me, letting out a nervous laugh. "Let's go sit down and have a drink."

I shoved him away and peered into the mirror, then turned to glare at Carter, who was trying hard not to laugh.

"I'm glad you find this amusing," I snorted.

"I'm not laughing," he struggled to say, "I'm sorry."

"There was a message on the mirror," I insisted, "someone is, or was, in here."

He lifted an eyebrow. "Someone broke into your apartment to write on your mirror?"

"There was a message!" I insisted.

"I'm sure there was," he laughed.

I angrily shoved past him and walked to the kitchen. "Next time you're wondering why I won't go out with you, remember this," I huffed.

"Oh, c'mon, Zo," he called after me as he retrieved the whiskey from the wall and followed me into the kitchen.

He set the bottle on the counter. "Tell you what, you pour us a couple glasses of this, and I'll look around again and double check that we're alone."

I cringed at the way he said the word 'alone,' but nodded anyway.

"I saw something in the mirror," I reaffirmed, scooping pasta into two bowls.

"Maybe it was a ghost," he teased.

The thought hadn't crossed my mind. I wasn't sure what scared me more, the idea of an intruder or an unwelcome visitor from another dimension.

"Is this building haunted?" I asked.

"Not that I know of," he replied as he checked the few rooms that made up my apartment.

He returned to the kitchen and stopped at the bar stools. "Nothing here," he confirmed.

"Thanks," I said, handing him a bowl of pasta.

"I'm sorry," he apologized. "You're right, I'm an asshole." He smirked, holding up his glass, "but I'm an asshole that brought whiskey."

I tried to hide my smile as I rolled my eyes at him.

"Here's to the ghost," he said, clinking his glass against mine.

I lifted the glass to my lips, and the flickering lights of the manor crossed my mind. *Could something have followed me home?* I quickly shook away the thought and downed the contents of my glass, wincing as the honey-flavored liquid stung my throat.

He held up his now empty glass. "Another?"

"I'll be so drunk if I have two shots before I eat," I countered.

"Fair enough," Carter said, helping himself to another glass of whiskey. He followed me into the living room, taking a small sip from his drink as he sat on the couch next to me. Wiping his upper lip with his hand, he grabbed the remote with the other and asked, "What do you want to watch?"

"You pick," I mumbled through a bite of food.

Proving he'd made no effort to get to know me over the past few years, Carter selected a horror movie. I said nothing as the title screen rolled, and Carter smiled. I struggled not to roll my eyes as I thought, *he totally thinks I'm going to get scared and cuddle up to him.*

As suspected, shortly into the movie, Carter set his bowl on the table in front of us and, less than casually, relaxed an arm over my shoulder.

After a moment of hesitation, I allowed myself to relax into his side and I had to admit, his warm, toned bicep around me did feel nice. *How bad can he be?* I snuggled into him for the rest of the movie.

As the end credits rolled, he asked, "Horror movies really don't scare you, huh?"

I sat up straight and turned to look him in the eye. "I told you my mom and I used to watch them every Halloween."

"Right," he hung his head in apology, "sorry."

"It's fine," I mumbled, looking away from him.

He leaned away from the backrest of the couch and softly brought his palm to my cheek. He gently turned my head to face him. "Let me make it up to you," he said before leaning in. For a split second, I considered turning away, but I decided against it. I'd never know how I really felt about him, if I didn't give him a chance. Our lips connected for the first time, and I struggled to find that tingling sensation that I'd experienced when Nolan had nearly kissed me. Carter deepened the kiss, and I sat motionless, letting him, willing myself to feel something for this man that so desperately wanted me to be his. I finally, gently, pushed away from him.

"It's getting late. I should get some sleep," I said.

He nodded with a smile as he rose from the couch, and asked, "Are we still on for our weekly bar crawl tomorrow?"

I nodded.

He left my apartment, and I listened for the sound of his front door latching for the night. Then, I lay in bed, staring at the ceiling as I wondered how it would've felt to kiss Nolan.

***

The following night, as promised, I hopped into a car with Carter and we rode downtown to begin our bar crawl.

At the third bar of the night, Carter ran into yet another "friend from the gym," and I retired to the bar for a drink while they played a game of pool. I leaned over the bar enough for the bartender to hear my order and then relaxed onto the bar stool. The bartender placed a lemon on the rim of a glass before pushing it toward me. I handed him a twenty, and he slid the cash off the bar and turned to the person on my left. I looked through the corner of my eye to see if I recognized the person who'd joined me at the bar. A dark-haired man sat beside me. I thought he looked familiar, but it was hard to tell without turning my head to get a better look.

When I did, I recognized him instantly. He smiled at me and asked, "Zoey, right?"

I set my glass down mid sip and quickly swallowed. "Nolan. Hi."

He gave the room a once over and leaned into me, sounding somewhat concerned. "You didn't come downtown alone did you?" he asked.

I shook my head and nervously sipped at my drink. Pointing toward the pool table, I explained, "I came with Carter, who, as you can see, is far more interested in his gym friends."

Nolan awkwardly lifted a beer to his lips, and I couldn't help but notice how they glistened from the moisture on the outside of the bottle. Distracted by the thought of our almost-kiss, I almost missed him asking, "So, how long have you and Carter been together?"

Drawn back to reality, I laughed. "We're just friends," I confirmed, more to myself than Nolan.

Before Nolan could reply, Cameron came up behind him, placed an arm around his shoulder and kissed him on the cheek. "We're just friends too," Cameron cooed.

"Go away," Nolan replied playfully, laughing as he threw Cameron's arm off of his shoulder.

Cameron giggled as he leaned over to hug me. "Hey Zoey, how's it going?"

"Good," I chimed, peering toward the pool table to make sure Carter hadn't noticed. Cameron and Carter had never gotten along.

Cameron ordered a beer from the bar and announced, "there's a ripped blonde guy over there just begging for the Cameron special." He winked at Nolan and raised his eyebrows teasingly as he whispered to Nolan, "don't forget to use protection."

We swiveled on our stools and watched as he stumbled toward an unsuspecting group of guys. We laughed, shaking our heads as we turned back to each other.

I struggled to come up with something to say, and he seemed to be having the same problem. He finally joked, "we've got nine months of freedom until we have to dress up again."

I smiled, "ugh, don't remind me it's so soon."

He admitted, "for what it's worth, I had a lot of fun with you at the manor."

I nodded. "Yeah, hanging out with you made the whole costume thing a little more tolerable," I agreed.

"Why do you hate it so much?" he wondered. "I mean, I don't like it, but you seem like you *really* hate it."

When I hesitated, he backtracked. "You don't have to answer that. I didn't mean to get personal."

"It's okay," I assured him. "My mom used to dress me in these ridiculous costumes when I was little and I always got made fun of for it."

As Nolan opened his mouth to respond, Carter placed his arm around me, and addressed Nolan a little too confidently, "Who are you?"

Nolan raised an eyebrow, trying to decide whether to get involved. I responded for him, "he's friends with Cameron." I slowly removed Carter's hand from my waist as I added, "we met at the manor."

Carter thought for a moment, sizing up my acquaintance and spat, "don't get any ideas bro, she's taken."

I scrunched my face, annoyed, and opened my mouth to respond, but he guided me off the stool and toward the door. I turned and shrugged an apology to Nolan as Carter led me out the door and ordered a ride on his phone. He placed his phone in his pocket and started to wrap his arms around me, pulling me into his chest.

I shoved him backward. "What is your problem?"

"My problem?" He pressed his chin to his chest as if my question confused him.

"We are not dating. Why would you tell him I'm taken?" I growled.

"We made out last night," he reminded me.

I rolled my eyes and groaned. "I've told you a million times Carter, I don't see you as anything more than a friend."

He scoffed, "well you have a funny way of showing it."

"It's not my fault you won't take no for an answer," I protested.

"It's not my fault you can't make up your mind," he spat back, "one second you say you're not interested, and the next we're making out on the couch. How am I supposed to take that?"

"Why can't you just accept that I don't want to date you," I huffed, throwing my hands in the air.

He let out a laugh of disbelief, shook his head and dropped his arms to his sides as he took two steps backward.

"You guys slept together at the party, didn't you?" he accused.

"Excuse me!" I scoffed.

"Just a guy you met at a party," he mocked. "Yeah, sure," he snorted as he began walking away.

I followed him and placed a hand on his shoulder as I caught up. "Carter..." I said.

He turned on his heels and held up his hands. "Just stop Zoey, I don't know why I bother with you. You always do this. Just when I think you're interested, you push me away."

I dropped my hand to my side and watched him get in a car, leaving me behind.

As I watched the car disappear around a corner, I thought back on the day I'd moved into our small apartment building. Without hesitation, Carter had come running out of his apartment to help me carry a table I was struggling with. That day really made it seem like we could put the past behind us and go back to the friendship we'd had before high school. The problem was, I just couldn't get past the way he'd treated me those years.

I sighed. *What am I supposed to do, force myself to feel something for him?*

I leaned against the building and rested my head on the bricks, staring at the stars. No matter how hard I tried to feel something for Carter, my mind would not let go of Nolan's face. I groaned, pulling my phone out and ordered a ride home.

Chapter 3

J ust as I had over the past few weeks, I walked into my apartment after another late-night shift with Carter's scornful gaze following me from his window. I sighed as I turned the key in the lock, telling myself not to give him the satisfaction of a glance. I entered my apartment, dropping my bag over the half-wall onto the couch, and yawned as I moved down the hall toward the bathroom.

I turned the hot water on in the shower and undressed before getting in. The warm condensation of the shower clung to the ornate Victorian mirror I'd picked up from a thrift store the day I moved in. I wrapped a towel around myself as I stepped out of the shower. Then, I used my palm to brush away the droplets, revealing a watery mess of mascara running down my cheek. I wet the hand towel that hung beside the door and used the towel to gently clean around my eyes. I stepped back to make sure that I'd gotten it all and froze as a girl in a Victorian dress stared back at me from the spot my reflection should've been. Her dark hair clinging to her cheeks, she made eye contact with me and I blinked a few times, unable to speak. I clutched my towel to my chest and willed her to say something, but just as quickly as she'd appeared, she was gone.

I cautiously dressed and sat on the couch to collect my thoughts. I wondered what to do, I could tell Carter, but with the state of our friendship hanging in limbo, I wasn't sure that was the best option. Besides, he'd probably just make fun of me. *Was it even real? It couldn't be...right?*

She looked just like the girl in the manor's paintings. I wanted to believe it was just my mind playing tricks, but it was hard to ignore after the tapping I'd heard the other day... *Could that have been her?*

I frantically searched my apartment over and over for the girl, to no avail. Staring into the mirror, I begged her to come back and prove I wasn't crazy. I didn't know what to do other than call the one person I thought might actually believe me, Cameron. The only reason I'd agreed to go to the manor in the first place was to satisfy his desire to experience the paranormal. As long as I'd known him, he strived to tell anyone he could about the ghost of a clown that lived in his attic as a child. I was sure he'd believe me. But even if he didn't, at the very least I knew I could trust his judgement if he said I was insane.

"I told you, Zoey, I'm not writing the accident report for you," Cameron joked on the other end of the line.

I couldn't help but laugh. Cameron always knew how to lighten the mood, even when I was terrified. I replied, "if I have to ask *you* to write my report, I have bigger worries than getting fired."

"Rude," he gasped, and I could picture his hand slapping his chest dramatically as he said it.

"Don't act like it's not true," I teased.

"I'm hurt Zoey," he pretended to sob long enough to elicit a laugh from me. He finally dropped the act and asked, "What's up?"

"I want to ask you something, but you can't make fun of me," I began.

"Oh, Zoey, I'm flattered, but you know I'm not into you like that," Cameron laughed.

"You're a pain in the ass," I replied.

I could picture the smile on his face as he replied, "sorry, couldn't resist. I'll be serious now."

"I think I just saw a ghost," I whispered.

"Really? Where?" He asked, excited.

"In my apartment," I explained, "Cam, she looked so real I thought it was a person, but I've looked through the apartment ten times. There's no one here."

"Did you recognize her?" Cameron inquired. "Was it your mom?"

"No, it wasn't her," I mumbled. I knew how crazy my next sentence would sound. I took a deep breath and revealed, "she looked like Martha Meridion."

"No way," he gasped. "Did you get her on film?"

I paused. There was nothing to show I hadn't hallucinated the entire thing. Maybe Carter was right about me seeing things. Maybe I am just stressed.

"Maybe I was just seeing things. I've been a little off since the fight with Carter," I said.

"Oh, screw Carter," Cameron groaned, "I can bring my video camera over and try to film her. I'll be famous for sure if I can catch an actual ghost on camera."

I sighed, "be my guest."

"I'll be there in an hour," he replied giddily, "tell Martha to wait for me."

"Will do," I laughed.

***

Cameron walked through the door about forty-five minutes later with his camera bag and huffed, "that prick needs to get a life."

I raised an eyebrow, and he explained, "your lovely neighbor came out on the porch for the sole purpose of accusing me of sleeping with you...again."

I dropped my shoulders and sighed in defeat, "just ignore him."

"Don't have to tell me twice," Cameron replied. "Any who, where's my beautiful subject?"

I led him to the bathroom and watched him film multiple angles. He took still photos on his phone and recorded questions that he asked to the empty room.

I leaned against the doorway sipping a glass of water. "Any luck?"

He shook his head in disappointment.

"Did you try offering her the Cameron special?" I joked.

He cracked a smile. "Some people just don't know what they're missing."

I rubbed his shoulder sympathetically. "If I see her again, I'll get her on camera for you."

"Thanks, Zoey," Cameron said, "I'm hungry, let's order food."

"Sure," I smiled, "the usual?"

He nodded, and I placed an online order for Chinese. "It'll be here in twenty-five minutes," I informed him.

"Cool," Cameron said, plopping onto the couch.

I could tell he wanted to talk about ghosts more, so I inquired, "What was the clown's name again?"

His face lit up, and he reminded me, "Toby. He lived in my old house years before we moved in. He went to clown college, but never got hired by the circus and he was so depressed he shot himself in the attic."

"Right, Toby," I nodded, "Didn't your dad hear him walking around one day?"

"Yeah, but to this day he swears it was a mouse in the attic," he scoffed, "like I can't tell the difference between a mouse and human footsteps."

"Did you ever catch Toby on camera?" I wondered.

"No, we moved years before I got my first camera," he pouted.

"Maybe someday when you're a famous ghost hunter, they'll let you in," I teased.

"They better." He smiled.

"Has Nolan mentioned anything to you about seeing ghosts since we were at the manor?" I asked.

He shook his head and rose from the couch to retrieve a beer from the fridge.

"Nah, Nolan doesn't believe in ghosts," Cameron replied, the light from the fridge illuminating his freckles.

"Why do you think she chose me?" I spoke louder so he could hear me.

The glass bottle clicked as he removed the top. "Maybe because you're nice. Local legend says her dad was kind of a douche. Maybe she wanted someone to talk to about it."

It was a reasonable enough explanation, but there were plenty of other women at the manor that night. "But why not one of the historians, like Ellie at the manor? Why me?"

He shrugged. "Who knows? Maybe she just likes you."

"What do you know about the Meridions?" I asked.

The doorbell rang, and Cameron opened the door to grab our food from the delivery driver. As he closed the door he replied, "not much, my dad's friend studies local history though. I can get you his number if you want to pick his brain."

If it really was Martha Meridion in my mirror, I wanted to know more. I nodded.

***

Cameron: Dr. Price's number is 725-544-8195.

   Zoey: Thanks!

I paced the living room, not sure how to present the situation to the professor. I was sure an intellectual, like himself, would think I was crazy if I told him I saw a ghost, I had to think of another way to get the answers I needed.

After a long moment of thought, I called him under the pretense of writing a research paper for a college class. He agreed to meet with me to tell me what he knew about the Meridions.

With asking Carter for a ride now out of the question, I ordered a ride to the university's history building to meet Dr. Price. I stepped onto the cracked white and black checkered tile of the atrium and took note of the musty smell of the old wood as I approached Dr. Price's office. His door was the last on the left side of a long hallway at the back of the building.

Pausing at the ancient looking wooden door labelled "Robert Price PHD", I fisted my hand to knock but hesitated, my knuckle almost touching it. I took a deep breath, taking note of the building's back door just to my right, the escape route I'd use if he didn't believe me. Then, I knocked twice.

"Come on in," a muffled voice spoke through the door. I looked at the doorknob and hovered my hand over it before turning it and allowing the door to fall open.

He immediately stopped typing at his computer and swiveled his chair to face me with a sincere smile. "Hello Zoey."

"Hi," I offered shyly.

"Please, have a seat," he motioned toward a chair across from him, "I was excited to have you contact me about this project. It's not often I get to dig into the Meridion's story."

I settled into my chair nervously and he added, "What about them piqued your interest?"

I wasn't sure if I should make something up, jump right into why I was there, or do something in between, "umm, Cameron..." I said.

"Ahh, yes, he's always had quite an affinity for the paranormal," he smiled.

My eyes widened anxiously, "uhh, he just...it's not like...I just wanted to find out about them."

He laughed, holding up his hand. "Don't worry, no judgement here."

I let my shoulders relax. Maybe he wouldn't think I was crazy after all.

"What can you tell me about Martha?" I asked.

He thought for a moment, "there's not much history on her...she was the couple's only child, she died young from TB. She was very close with her aunt and uncle," he paused, "which Landon wasn't too pleased about."

"Why?" I asked.

"Landon and Reginald never got along much," he replied, "at least according to the historians."

"Did they live at the manor?" I wondered.

"They did for a while. Until Martha's aunt, Loretta, died during childbirth in 1987. Her uncle lived in the manor until his disappearance in 1908."

"Disappearance?" I asked, letting my curiosity take hold of the conversation.

He shook his head. "No one knows what happened to him. Some say he took off down south, others believe he died in a work-related accident. Some even think Landon Meridion killed him."

He laughed, seeming to find the last theory amusing.

I thought for a moment. "What do *you* think happened?"

He shrugged. "I'd tend to say he likely skipped town. We're talking over a hundred years ago. If either of the other theories were true, surely someone would have found the body by now."

I nodded. *Interesting.* "What happened to the rest of the family?"

"Her mother Edith's, mental illness became overwhelming shortly after his disappearance. Landon had Edith committed to Susquehanna State Asylum," he explained. "According to the stories, when her uncle disappeared, Martha was beside herself and set out into the orchard in search of her uncle. Landon found her shivering in the pouring rain. She never recovered from the pneumonia that followed."

"I thought she died of tuberculosis?" I asked, remembering what I'd read in her room.

He smiled. "There is a lot of discussion regarding how she died. Some say TB. Some say pneumonia. I've also heard people suggest she died of hypothermia. Unfortunately, Landon refused an autopsy, so we'll never know for sure," he explained.

"The plaque also said her mirror was given to her by her uncle Reginald. Do you know anything about that?" I inquired.

I could tell I'd piqued his interest. He replied, "well, Zoey, I'm not much of a believer, but according to some it's a haunted mirror. Lady Perida investigated it once. Legend has it, she saw Landon's face in the mirror."

I froze, remembering the flickering lights and the breeze in Martha's room.

He smiled. "I'm going to guess you saw him too?"

I was too shocked to speak.

He reached into the top drawer of his desk for a pen and wrote something on a piece of paper before handing it to me.

"This is the address of Lady Perida's shop. She's far more qualified in this department than I am. Pay her a visit, she may be able to get you the answers you're looking for," he said.

"Thanks," I whispered, taking the paper from him. I stared at the notecard and steadily rose from my seat before quietly leaving his office.

***

Back at my apartment, I sat on the couch with my laptop and began researching Lady Perida. Over the course of a few hours, I determined that she was a local psychic who'd claimed to have had an experience at the manor about ten years ago. According to an article, the experience was so traumatic that she would never agree to step foot in the manor again. Another newspaper article I found claimed that the majority of townspeople didn't believe her and that her case to have the manor professionally cleansed was dropped swiftly.

What did she see? I wondered.

I decided I had to find out, but I wasn't ready to talk to Lady Perida quite yet. So I texted Cameron instead.

Zoey: I think I'm going to get tickets for the Valentine's Day party at the manor. Wanna come?

Cameron: Duh! Everyone knows Valentine's parties are the best places to meet people.

Zoey: Yeah, okay LOL

Cameron: Cameron special coming right up ;)

Zoey: Eww

Cameron: Nolan will be there ;)

Zoey: OMG, I told you I'm not looking for a relationship.

Cameron: Uh huh, is that why you were all over him?

Zoey: I was not!

Chapter 4

I hopped out of Cameron's car, and the two of us walked together toward the manor. I wore my favorite off-the-shoulder cream sweater and Cameron sported a pink short-sleeved button down with red hearts all over it. Cameron held the door for me, and I stepped into the foyer where Nolan stood in a grey V-neck.

"Hey, Cam!" Nolan side-hugged him.

I nervously met Nolan's gaze, and he hugged me. "Nice to see you again."

I nodded shyly, and replied, "you, too."

As the room filled with people, the three of us stood off to the side, awaiting the welcome speech. The woman from the Halloween party sashayed into the center of the room in a red and blue gown that matched the siding of the manor almost exactly.

She clapped twice.

"Hello, hello," she sang, "as you all know it is Valentine's Day, or as we at the manor like to call it, anti-Valentine's Day. As I'm sure most of you know, the Meridion's despised this holiday, for it is the day on which their beloved daughter passed away."

I looked at Nolan and Cameron to see if they'd react to the statement. Nolan's eyes met mine, and he leaned into me. "Did you know that?"

I shook my head as the woman continued, "Landon Meridion scheduled the funeral for that same afternoon. It took place right over there."

She pointed to where the three of us stood, and I felt a breeze nudge my hair.

"Since that day, the Meridion's hosted an anti-Valentine's Day party each year in remembrance of Martha. I ask that you all show respect throughout the night. Perhaps, if you're lucky, she'll stop by and say hello."

With that, she excused the group and left us to explore the manor.

"Drink time," Cameron announced, grabbing mine and Nolan's hands, leading us toward the kitchen.

We each acquired a drink, clinked our glasses together, and said, "to anti-Valentine's Day."

Cameron chugged his glass and picked up the ladle of jungle juice to refill it. Taking a sip, he announced, "hot brunette guy, two o'clock."

As he started to walk away, he turned to whisper, "don't wait up for me."

I laughed as I turned to face Nolan and said, "I guess it's you and me tonight."

"I'm okay with that," he admitted.

We wandered into the family room to stand by the fireplace.

"How have you been?" Nolan asked.

"Good. Nothing new really, just go to work, come home and cook." I shrugged.

"You still seeing that guy, Carter?" he asked.

I rolled my eyes. "No, and I never was," I reminded him.

He sipped his drink and replied, "he sure seemed to think you were."

"He wishes," I scoffed, before changing the subject. "How is school going?"

"Good. We just finished World War One, now onto World War Two. Super exciting," he joked.

"Riveting," I sarcastically replied.

I stepped back from the fire, tripping over a chair, and Nolan held out an arm to stop my fall. I placed my hand on his chest for security and looked at him.

"Thanks," I said as he continued to hold me.

I became aware of the heaviness of my breathing as I looked into his dark brown eyes longingly. With a sigh, we both dropped our hands and took a step back from one another.

"Want to go explore the manor?" I offered, cutting the tension.

"Sure," he smiled, following me toward the spiral staircase.

We ascended the stairs until we came to a long hallway with ornate sconces lining the wall on either side. At the end of the hall, we found an opened door that revealed a large room with teal striped wallpaper. The sconces flickered as I stepped through the doorway onto the walnut floors.

"They really need to hire an electrician," Nolan commented, reading my mind.

"Maybe it's the ghost of Martha coming to haunt you for not believing in her," I teased.

"Will you hold my hand if I get scared?" he joked back.

"Only if you promise not to squeeze too hard," I replied, taking in the room.

The room was much larger than Martha's, with a king-size bed, two nightstands and a large wardrobe on the left wall. On the right side of the room, a floor-to-ceiling bookshelf filled with ancient looking books towered over a card table and chair with a teal cushion. I approached the bookshelf and awed at the stacks.

"I've always wanted a library like this," I said.

Nolan agreed, "it is pretty cool."

"Do you read?" I gestured toward him with my glass.

He shrugged. "Sometimes. Mostly non-fiction."

"I'm more of a fantasy person, myself," I said.

"What can I say? I'm a history nerd," he replied.

A noise emitted from the shelf to our right, and our heads turned toward the sound.

"What was that?" I wondered out loud.

Nolan finished his drink. "Probably just the house. Old houses make noise."

I nodded in agreement, but I wasn't convinced. As Nolan scanned the titles on the shelf, I eyed the right side of the room for clues as to what had made the sound.

A black leather-bound book sticking slightly out of alignment with the others caught my attention and I walked toward it, removing it from the shelf.

I read the front out loud, "Families of the Lackawanna Railroad."

"Oh, sounds very compelling," Nolan joked.

I couldn't help the smile that spread across my face as I skimmed the pages. I stopped on one that piqued my interest.

"Arthur Meridion's dynasty," I read aloud.

Nolan leaned over to me and taunted, "maybe Arthur Meridion is haunting us."

I lowered the book and thought about the girl in the mirror. I looked at Nolan.

"If I tell you something, do you promise not to laugh?" I asked.

He shrugged. "Sure."

I took a deep breath, allowing the book to close on my thumb. "This is going to sound crazy," I admitted.

He raised an eyebrow. "Okay."

I sighed. "I think Martha Meridion is trying to contact me."

I waited for him to laugh, but he didn't. I continued, "I saw a girl in the mirror at my apartment, and she looked just like the girl in the portrait downstairs."

He took in my words. "I've been having some weird things happen too," he professed.

"Really?" I replied, relieved.

"The other day I came home from work and the lights in my kitchen would not stop flickering. I didn't think much of it at first, but then a book fell off my shelf while I was watching TV," he recounted.

He paused and pointed to the book in my hands. "And get this...the book that fell was about the history of the Meridion family, just like this one."

My eyes widened in disbelief. "What? That's crazy."

He nodded. "I didn't even tell Cam because I knew he'd jump all over the ghost thing, but there's just something about this house..." he trailed off.

I looked around the room and then at the book in my hand.

"I told Cam about the girl in the mirror," I admitted.

"Did he ask you to film it?" Nolan assumed.

"Of course," I replied. "But he also encouraged me to talk to this professor at Meridion College about it."

"Did you?" He inquired.

I nodded. "The professor said that ghosts can appear in mirrors. Maybe if we go back to her room and look at her mirror, we can find out what is going on," I suggested.

He nodded, and I slid the book back onto the shelf before following him out of the study. We made our way to the mint-colored room and stopped in front of the mirror.

"It looks like a normal mirror to me," Nolan commented.

I sighed, looking around the room. Nothing seemed out of place. I looked into the mirror and met Nolan's eyes in his reflection.

"Your eyes look really nice with that shirt," he breathed.

I blushed, looking down at my sweater.

"Thanks," I said, twisting the ends of my hair so the curls fell perfectly on either side of my face.

He smirked, letting a gust of air escape his nose.

"What?" I wondered, turning to face him.

His hand drifted toward my face, allowing it to rest on my cheek before moving closer.

Tickles of electricity flowed through me, but I couldn't bring myself to close the distance. How could I after rejecting Carter claiming I didn't want a relationship? And I didn't. Right?

He pulled back, resting his forehead on mine, and we both laughed nervously.

I turned to look at the floor, trying to hide the rosy warmth invading my cheeks.

Looking back at him, I couldn't help but admit, "I'm really drunk."

Sorry, I didn't mean to take advantage," he said, almost in a panic.

I shook my head. "It's okay. I just don't want you to think..." I paused, trying to collect my thoughts. "I'm just not really interested in a relationship right now," I wasn't sure who I was trying to convince, me, or him.

He shrugged. "I'm good with friends."

"Thanks," I smiled.

He pulled his phone from his pocket and held it out to me.

"Maybe we can hang out sometime?" he asked, "as friends."

I took the phone from him and nodded, typing my name and number into the device before handing it back to him.

He turned to face the mirror once more and held his camera up to it. "Let's take a picture for your contact card."

I smiled into the phone as he snapped the photo. He clicked to view the image.

"Dang it, I suck at taking pictures," he griped.

He turned the phone to show me the photo, and I noticed a white mass blocking a portion of each of our reflections.

"Let me try," I said, taking the phone from him and snapping another photo.

I showed him the picture, which was perfectly clear, and he shrugged. "Like I said, I suck at taking pictures."

We inspected the mirror some more and couldn't find anything that looked off.

Nolan stared at my reflection and finally said, "I think it's just an old mirror."

"Yeah, you're right," I gave in, "let's go find Cam."

Chapter 5

The following weekend, I sat on the couch in my apartment, my feet resting on the coffee table, sipping at a glass of wine. I closed my eyes, allowing myself to relax, and rested the base of the glass on my thigh.

Glass shattered in the kitchen, yanking me out of my repose. I jumped from the couch, nearly spilling the red liquid in my glass, and ran to the kitchen. I scanned the countertops and floor, finding nothing out of place. I opened and closed each cabinet and the dishwasher, still nothing.

I turned to face the bedroom and inspected it before searching the remainder of the apartment for the source of the sound. Nothing. I returned to the living room and gulped down the remainder of the wine.

I walked into the bathroom and set the glass on the vanity. Resting my hands on either side of the sink, I stared into my reflection. *Maybe Carter was right. Maybe I should talk to someone about this.*

I shook off the thought and lifted my left hand to the faucet to turn the water on. Leaning over the sink, I ran my hands through the water, then wet my face. I grabbed a moss-green towel from the hook to my right and began to pat the water away. As I moved the towel across my face, I could've sworn I saw something in the mirror. I let the towel fall to the floor and locked my gaze on the mirror. There was nothing there. *I need to know what is happening. I need to talk to Ellie from the historical society.*

I collected my wallet and phone, then headed out to the parking lot to meet my ride. As oak trees passed by the window, I ran through the upcoming conversation in my head.

So, I think Martha Meridion is haunting me.

That sounded ridiculous.

Has anyone ever reported being haunted by Martha?

This woman is going to have me committed.

I took a deep breath as the car stopped outside the manor. A black and white sign hung from the front door knocker, indicating that the manor was accepting visitors. I pushed the door open and looked around the lobby.

"Hello dear," Ellie Fadra happily greeted me.

"Hi," I said shyly.

"Welcome to Meridion Manor," she said, "I'm Ellie, the head of the historical society."

"Yeah, I know you. I've been to a few of the parties here," I replied.

"How lovely," she replied with a smile. "Would you like a tour?"

"Umm," I hesitated, "actually, I was hoping to talk to someone about the history of the manor. I have a few questions."

Her face lit up. "Oh, wonderful. I love it when students write about the manor. It truly doesn't get the attention it deserves."

I elected to let her believe I was a student. It was easier than trying to explain the real reason I'd come.

"What aspect of the family is your report about?" she asked.

"I'm looking for information about Martha Meridion."

Her smile brightened as she replied, "my favorite member of the Meridion family. Right this way."

She led me into the parlor, where the fire crackled below the family portrait that I'd noticed the night of the Halloween party.

"Have a seat." She motioned toward a raspberry pink chair as she filled two mugs with tea. I hesitated before sitting down, it was the same chair that had caused the butler to trip that night.

Setting the mugs on the table in front of me, she sat on a chair to my right.

"So, tell me what you already know, and then I'll fill in the blanks," she proposed.

"I really don't know much," I admitted. "I know she's the daughter of the couple that owned the manor, and I read the plaque on the mirror upstairs."

She shook her head in disapproval. "It really is a shame. The history of the manor is so rich and they don't bother to teach a thing about it."

With a huff she continued, "well I suppose there's no one better than me to explain it anyhow. I am, after all, the president of the historical society."

I nodded politely. "Could you give me a brief history of the family?"

She smiled and took a sip from her mug before beginning, "Arthur Meridion was an astute businessman, far ahead of his time. He had the foresight to purchase the property before the railroads were even built."

"I thought his name was Landon?" I asked.

She laughed. "Oh silly, Arthur is Landon and Reginald's father. When his oldest son, Landon, married Edith, Arthur gifted the manor to them."

I nodded. Then she stood from the couch and made her way to a window overlooking the back of the house. She turned her head to indicate that I should follow.

"Out this window here, you can sort of see, the railroad tracks run right through the center of the orchard. The state agreed to pay a hefty sum to Landon when he agreed to it."

I peered out at the long-forgotten tracks overrun with grass. "I would've been pissed if I were Reginald," I commented.

She held up a finger as if to tell me to have patience. "I'll get to him in a moment. Follow me."

With that, she spun toward the atrium and I followed as she ascended the spiral staircase.

Talking over her shoulder, she continued. "When Arthur died in 1881, he left his fortune to his two sons Landon and Reginald. Of course the manor was already Landon's, so to keep the peace, Landon allowed Reginald and his wife to live in the house free of charge."

We paused at the top of the stairs, and a door squeaked.

"Don't mind the doors, it's an old house, things move," she said, then continued, "now, to backtrack a bit, Arthur's wife, Ester, adored Halloween. So each year they'd hold a Halloween ball, inviting all the regional businessmen and their families. In particular, he'd invite their daughters, in hopes that his two boys would find wives."

Waving for me to follow her, she proceeded down the hallway. "Reginald and Landon set their eyes on one of the young ladies at the ball and an argument ensued. Now, Arthur, being the respected businessman he was, could not have his sons embarrassing him by arguing over a woman. He arranged for Ms. Sullivan to marry his eldest son."

"Oh my gosh," I whispered. "That's terrible. Shouldn't she have gotten a choice in the matter?"

"Indeed," she agreed. "Reginald was furious. He married Loretta Bauer, the daughter of his father's nemesis, taking her name when he did, just to spite his father. From that day forward, he was known as Reginald Bauer."

I followed Ellie into Martha's room, and she paused in front of the mirror. "Now, Martha Meridion, the couple's daughter, loved her Uncle Reginald. She was quite often scolded by Landon for speaking to him. On her 21st birthday, she received this mirror as a gift from him. Reginald disappeared shortly after."

"Is the mirror haunted?" I asked.

She laughed. "Oh, I don't think so, dear."

A bit disappointed, I paused before asking, "What happened to Reginald?"

Ellie shrugged. "It depends on who you ask. Some say he skipped town, others believe he could be buried on these very grounds. Of course, nothing has ever been proven."

"Haven't they searched the property?" It seemed obvious to me.

She sighed. "They couldn't. You see, Landon owned the property, and he refused to have a search party on the land without compelling cause. Martha put up quite the fuss at first, but Landon agreed to let her remain in the manor and another word was not heard about the disappearance of her uncle."

"What do *you* think happened to him?" I hoped she'd have a better answer than Dr. Price.

She shook her head and shrugged. "If you ask me, I think Landon Meridion killed him."

"But no one has ever found the body?" I confirmed what Dr. Price had told me.

"For what it's worth, no one has really looked for it," she revealed.

She looked out the window and scoffed, "I'm certainly not trekking through that orchard."

I looked out at the thousands of trees spread across the property and an eerie feeling consumed me as I thought about the secrets that could be hidden among them.

"You think his body is in the orchard?" I asked.

"The railroad was still under construction when he disappeared, it'd be a great place to hide a body if you ask me," she replied.

"I guess it's not like anyone in those days would risk tearing up the tracks to find out," I replied.

"Precisely," Ellie agreed. "Too expensive and too time consuming. I think most people were just glad to be rid of the Meridion's problem child."

Would Landon really have killed his brother? I wondered as I looked out at the apple trees, which were engulfed by a cloudy mist.

I shook off the grotesque thought and looked at the family portrait on the wall.

"So how did Martha get sick?" I asked.

Ellie looked sad. "Her mother went crazy, and they admitted her to the asylum up north. I'd like to think it's because she knew the truth about Reginald. I've always believed that she had a place in her heart for him even after her marriage to Landon. Officially, historians believe that it was the death of Edith's sister that led to her demise."

I nodded, staring out the window at the vast orchard behind the manor. There must've been hundreds of miles of trees.

"But to answer your question, Martha was devastated by the loss of her uncle," Ellie explained, "and the loss of her mother just made it worse. No one told Martha where her mother had gone, just that she wouldn't be coming back. It's said she contracted pneumonia while attempting to search for her mother in the orchard.

She looked around the familiar mint-green room. "This, of course, is Martha's bedroom. I'm sure you remember from the parties."

I nodded, studying the intricacies of the ornate molding until she spoke again.

Pointing toward the mirror, she said, "this mirror belonged to Martha."

I interrupted her. "I heard people have seen Martha in the mirror. Is that true?"

She waved away the comment. "I've heard people say they've seen things around the manor, but never Martha, specifically. It's all stories if you ask me. Some say I'm a skeptic. I say I'm realistic."

"You don't believe in ghosts either?" I asked, starting to wonder if Cameron and I were the only ones that did.

Ellie replied, "if you're looking for ghost stories, I suggest you talk to Lady Perida downtown."

I nodded and looked down at my watch. "I should probably get home. Thank you."

She smiled. "Of course, anytime."

***

Zoey: Wanna go to Lady Perida's with me after work tomorrow?

Cameron: Finally agreeing to that buy one, get one reading?

I chose to ignore his comment. He'd been trying for months to get me to agree to a psychic reading.

Zoey: Dr. Price and Ellie both told me she might be able to tell us more about the girl in the mirror.

Cameron: I love a good seance. I'm so in!

***

After our shift at O'Connell's, I walked with Cameron to the parking lot. As we approached his car, I noticed Nolan leaning against the passenger door.

"Uh, hey Nolan," I said, looking at Cameron for an explanation.

"Let's talk in the car," Cameron said, shivering. "It's freezing out here."

Nolan got into the front seat and turned to address me. "Cam said you wanted to join us for pizza and a movie tonight."

I glared at Cameron through the rearview mirror, and he smirked.

Well played Cam.

"Actually, I thought it would be fun to go talk to Lady Perida first," I replied.

Nolan raised an eyebrow. "He's got you on the buy one, get one thing too?"

"He's relentless. But no. I'm convinced Martha Meridion is trying to contact me, and I need to know why," I said confidently.

Cameron stopped at a red light and turned to look at me. "What makes you think it's Martha and not just some random ghost?"

The car began to move again. "I told you. I saw her."

Cameron proceeded to fill Nolan in, unaware that I'd already revealed it to him. "She saw a ghost in the mirror at her apartment. I tried to get it to show itself to me too, but it wouldn't."

Nolan raised an eyebrow skeptically. "And was this before or after a bottle of wine?" he joked.

Cameron rolled his eyes, and I sighed, looking out the window.

Now we both sound crazy.

As if he'd read my mind, Cameron perked up. "Maybe she's crazy, maybe not. But if anyone can tell us it's Lady Perida."

Nolan scoffed. "I don't know if listening to a psychic is a great way to prove your sanity."

"Thanks," I muttered from the backseat.

He turned to look at me, his expression soft. "I'm not saying you're crazy. I'm just saying it's a lot easier to believe your mind was playing tricks on you than to believe you saw a ghost." Then, he added, "Plus, aren't ghosts supposed to like haunt the place where they died? It's not like Martha died in your apartment."

Cameron replied. "I mean, in theory. But who's to say. There's so much we don't know about the afterlife."

"Or lack thereof," Nolan commented.

I sat up in my seat. "You really think we just cease to exist?" I asked him.

Nolan shrugged, and Cameron eyed him for a counter-argument as he shifted the car into park.

"I don't really know," Nolan admitted.

"No one does," Cameron replied, "that's the whole point."

Leaving the conversation behind, we stepped out of the car and followed the sidewalk past shops until we came to a small store with paisley tapestries covering the windows. A small A-frame sign indicated that the shop offered psychic readings. Nolan pulled the door open and held it as Cameron and I entered. The room was lit by a menagerie of white candles haphazardly strewn throughout the room. The scent of burning sage overwhelmed my nostrils as we made our way past various colored crystals and star pendants.

"Welcome, dears," a hoarse female voice spoke as a frail woman emerged from behind a tapestry featuring phases of the moon.

The woman walked with an amethyst-colored cane. Her loose fitting long sleeve dress complimented it perfectly and her graying tan hair frizzed from a lazily placed bun at the back of her head.

I smiled at her and Cameron spoke, "hello, we're here to get some help with a haunting."

"I know." She replied, looking at me. "Spirits are quite particular about who they choose to contact. I wouldn't take the responsibility lightly if I were you."

I looked at Cameron cautiously, and he said, "I told you she's the real deal."

I spoke up then, "Do you know why Martha chose me?"

She raised the hand that wasn't holding her cane and motioned for us to follow her as she disappeared behind the moon tapestry.

I turned to Cameron and then Nolan. The three of us shrugged in unison and followed her into the back room, Cameron leading the way.

Lady Perida stood in the center of a square ornamental rug. "Sit. In a circle," she instructed us.

Cameron and I obeyed, but she stopped Nolan, pointing at him with her cane. "You. Be a dear and help me sit."

Nolan set her cane to the side, and she shifted her weight to his shoulders as he guided her to the rug. She gestured for him to have a seat, then held her hands palm up on either knee. Cameron and I each joined one of our hands with hers and then joined hands with a reluctant Nolan to form a circular connection.

Cameron and Lady Perida closed their eyes as if they were meditating. Nolan and I looked at each other for guidance.

Lady Perida spoke, "Martha, are you here with us?"

Silence followed and Nolan's eye remained locked to mine.

She opened her eyes, a glimmer of panic in them, and let go of our hands. "Martha won't be speaking with us."

I raised an eyebrow. "So that's it?"

Nolan laughed uncomfortably, and Cameron huffed in disappointment.

Lady Perida turned to me. "As I said, spirits are very particular about who they speak with. If she's trying to communicate with you, I'm sure there's a good reason, but you'll have to figure it out on your own."

She then turned to Nolan. "And you, I suggest you refrain from further investigation. You have no idea what you're up against."

Cameron and I looked at Nolan, perplexed.

He admitted, "I may have seen something too."

My eyes widened. "You saw her?"

"Not exactly..." he hesitated. "I...I thought I saw a man standing in my kitchen."

Cameron and I stared at him in disbelief as he continued, "I didn't want to say anything because I thought I must've been seeing things."

I swatted his arm. "You acted like I was insane in the car!"

His face fell. "I didn't mean to Zoey, I just..."

I finished for him, understanding where he was coming from, "you didn't want to admit that you were crazy."

"I don't know what to believe anymore," he admitted.

Lady Perida took in our reactions. "I suggest you two," she pointed at Nolan and I, "refrain from meddling in things you don't understand."

"What don't we understand?" I pried.

She shook her head. "The Meridion manor is off limits for me. You want to mess with the secrets it contains, you'll be doing it alone."

With that, she held her arm toward the door. "It was lovely meeting you all, but I must prepare for my next appointment."

Cameron sighed in disappointment as he led the way out of the shop. Nolan placed an arm around his shoulder. "Don't take it personally, Cam. She's just a grumpy old lady," he said.

Cameron groaned, "every time I think I'm close to finding proof of the paranormal, I hit a roadblock."

Nolan squeezed his shoulder. "How about you pick tonight's movie?"

Chapter 6

We reflected on our visit to Lady Perida as we walked through town back to Cameron's car.

Nolan sulked beside me. "What kind of psychic can't contact a ghost?"

"She did contact it," Cameron spat, "it just didn't want to talk to us.

I turned to Nolan as we walked. "I can't believe you didn't tell us that you were having experiences."

He raised his hands in an exaggerated shrug. "It was probably just some faulty electric playing tricks on my eyes."

Cameron and I stopped in front of him. "Faulty wiring made a man appear in your kitchen?"

Nolan sighed. "Guys, c'mon, ghosts aren't real. It was probably just a shadow from outside or something."

"There's no window in your kitchen," Cameron countered.

With a sudden burst of courage, I challenged Nolan, "maybe we should go to your apartment and see this shadow for ourselves."

Cameron perked up at the idea. "I have my camera with me," he said.

"If you wanted to come to my house, you could just ask, you know," he said, winking at me.

"Hey," Cameron said, opening his car door. "There's only room for one lady's man in this car."

"I have no need to go to your apartment," I assured him from the backseat. "This is purely for research purposes."

***

Nolan sat at his dining room table with Cameron and I eagerly peering over his shoulder at his laptop screen.

"Search, how to conduct a seance," Cameron said, pointing toward the search bar.

I watched as Nolan typed. He leaned into the screen as he scrolled through the results.

"It says we'll need a Ouija Board and some candles," Nolan mumbled as he read the page he'd clicked on.

"I have a Ouija Board at my apartment," Cameron said, picking up his keys.

He moved to the door before Nolan and I had a chance to protest. "I'll be right back," he said, shutting the door behind him.

I took a seat next to Nolan at the table, and he looked at me. "I guess it's just the two of us."

Choosing to ignore his comment, I slid my chair closer to him so that I could see his laptop screen better.

"Does it say anything about how to actually perform the seance?" I asked.

He scrolled through the web page until he came to a list of questions. "There's a list of recommended questions to ask," he replied.

We scanned the page together, and I pointed to the right side of the screen. "There. How to use a Ouija Board."

The cursor moved to the side of the screen and Nolan read, "sit in a circle and place the board in between you."

I read the next line, "each player gently places a finger on the planchet."

Nolan continued, "ask a question and wait for a response."

I breathed out the last line of instructions, "the planchet will move to the answer."

"How are we going to know if Cam moves the planchet just to mess with us?" Nolan asked, holding his palms to the ceiling.

The lights began to flicker in the kitchen, and Nolan eyed me. "See. Faulty wiring."

I stood and moved toward the kitchen, my heart pounding. Just like that day in my apartment, it felt as if something was watching me. My eyes scanned the countertop and cabinets for anything amiss. I flicked the light switch off and then back on. The flickering stopped.

I returned to the table. "You should really call your landlord about that. It could start a fire," I suggested.

He sighed, "Trust me, I've tried. He keeps claiming there's nothing wrong with it."

"Have you tried taking a video to show him?" I asked.

Nolan looked at me with raised eyebrows. "Of course I did. He claimed I had Cameron edit the lighting."

"What?" I laughed. "That's ridiculous."

The sound of the front door swinging opened startled us both. I placed my hand on my heart and Nolan thrust his arm in front of me protectively.

"Damn, dude, you scared the crap out of me," Nolan said, dropping his arm as Cameron set a box down on the table. "Ever heard of knocking?"

Cameron laughed. "You know me, I like to make an entrance."

"Clearly," I huffed a sigh of relief.

Nolan reached for the box to unpack the board as I caught Cameron up on our research. "So we found a guide on how to use the board, and we found a list of questions to ask it."

"Sweet," Cameron replied, "dibs on asking if it's single."

I rolled my eyes. "Do you ever think about anything other than getting laid?"

"Not really," he shrugged, and we all laughed.

Cameron rubbed his hands together. "Let's get to it. I'm ready to talk to some ghosts."

Nolan rolled his eyes and carried the board to the living room. We sat cross-legged on the grey carpet, the board in the center of our circle.

"Everyone, place one finger gently on the planchet," I instructed, allowing my index finger to touch the wooden game piece.

Nolan and Cameron followed suit and looked at me for further instruction. I shrugged. "What should we ask it?"

Cameron pursed his lips and moved them off to one side of his face in thought. "Is Nolan's apartment haunted?"

With our eyes glued to the planchet, we waited for something to happen.

When the planchet didn't move, Nolan spoke, "Is the wiring in my apartment faulty?"

The planchet shook ever so slightly under my fingers and then slowly slid across the board to the top corner, resting on the word, "no."

Nolan tilted his head. "Very funny, Cam."

Cameron threw his hands up. "Dude, that wasn't me."

They both looked at me and I shook my head, my eyes wide with shock.

"Ask it something else," Cameron suggested, setting his finger back on the game piece.

Nolan sighed in defeat, humoring us. "Why are my lights flickering?"

The planchet didn't move.

I decided to play along, using one of the suggested questions from the website. "Is someone here with us?"

The game piece vibrated once again, and we watched it move to the opposite side of the board.

"Yes," I read out loud.

We eyed each other suspiciously, none of us were convinced that the piece was moving on its own. Suddenly, the chandelier above us dimmed and Cameron groaned. "Oh man, I forgot the candles."

I couldn't help but let out an amused breath as we stared at the ceiling. Cameron once again broke the silence. "*Who* is here with us?"

The bathroom door swung closed with a bang. We turned our heads toward the sound and sprung to our feet. Nolan placed a protective arm around me, and I moved my hand to rest on his chest. The sound of movement behind us caused us to turn, and we watched as the planchet slid across the board.

"Goodbye," Cameron whispered.

We stood frozen in shock until Nolan whispered. "You guys saw that, right?"

I nodded slowly, swallowing my fear, and Cameron pointed to the board. "I told you I wasn't moving it."

The three of us stood in place for a moment, allowing our heartbeats to return to normal. Nolan dropped his arm from my waist, and I removed mine from his chest.

"Now what?" He asked.

Cameron looked at his watch. "I should get going. I took a morning shift tomorrow. Maybe we try again tomorrow?"

"You're just going to leave?" Nolan stared at him wide-eyed.

He shrugged, placing a hand on my shoulder. "Zoey can keep you company."

"Thanks," I muttered sarcastically as he moved to retrieve his jacket from the wooden chair it was resting on.

"See you guys later," Cameron cheered as he closed the front door behind him.

Nolan took a deep breath and looked at me. "I have wine. We could watch a movie," he suggested.

I looked toward the bathroom door, still shaken from the game. I let out a shaky breath and replied with a nod. "Fine, but no horror movies."

Nolan moved to the kitchen, and I followed him, looking left to peek at the bathroom door as I stepped into the scarlet kitchen. Nolan opened the fridge and pulled out a blue bottle.

"Chardonnay?" he asked with a smile, and I could tell he remembered me saying it was my favorite.

I nodded, and he procured two glasses from a cedar cabinet, filling them each. He handed a glass to me and clinked his against it. "To the ghost."

I laughed while taking a sip and he looked toward the living room. "What movie should we watch?"

I shrugged. "You pick."

He nodded and led me toward the couch. Sitting down, he held out his arm so that I could snuggle into him, then rested his hand on my shoulder when I did. He picked up the remote and navigated to movie selections, deciding on a comedy film. I relaxed into his shoulder, sipping at my wine as we watched the movie.

When the movie ended, Nolan turned off the television, and I looked up at him, my head still resting on his shoulder.

"I should probably get home," I said.

He nodded, reluctantly, then remembered that I didn't have a car.

"I'll drop you off," he offered.

Chapter 7

When our shift ended the next day, Cameron drove us to Nolan's apartment.

"So, you and Nolan?" Cameron questioned me as he drove.

"Me and Nolan what?" I asked, pretending not to have any idea what he was asking.

"Oh, c'mon Zoey, you guys are totally a thing," he replied.

"We *totally* are not," I mocked him.

"Why not?" he asked. "You guys were so cute together at the party."

"What about you and Jaime?" I deflected.

"I'll tell you, if you tell me?" he said with a wink.

I rolled my eyes. "Every time I like a guy, he ends up liking someone else. Look what happened with Carter," I explained.

"Carter is an idiot," Cameron replied. "He only wanted Hana because she was the head cheerleader."

"I don't know," I muttered, wondering if maybe it was worth giving Nolan a chance.

"So, spill the tea," I changed the subject. "What's the deal with you and Jaime?"

Cameron parked the car and smirked. "I don't kiss and tell," he said, getting out of the car and racing to ring Nolan's doorbell.

"Not fair!" I yelled after him.

We stood, shivering in the lightly falling snow, as we waited for Nolan to open the door.

Finally, the door swung open, and Cameron complained as he shoved Nolan aside to get through the doorway. "Dude, it's freezing. Let me in."

We each greeted Nolan with a hug after removing our soaking wet shoes.

"Any ghost sightings last night?" Cameron inquired, setting his jacket on the back of a dining room chair.

"Not since we put the Ouija board away," Nolan replied, shaking his head.

"I brought my video camera," Cameron said, holding up the device, "maybe we can catch your ghost in the act."

"Don't ghosts only show up in the dark?" I questioned.

Cameron glared at me. "You watch too many movies."

He pulled a tripod from his backpack, which was sitting on the same chair his jacket was hung over, and began securing the camera to it.

As he twisted the camera into place, Nolan asked him, "Where are you putting that?"

Cameron winked and glanced at Nolan's bedroom. "Wherever you want me to."

"You're a pig," I groaned.

Nolan smiled in amusement. "I can assure you nothing has happened in that room in a while."

Cameron looked from Nolan to me with a smirk. "Since last night?"

I glared at him. "We watched a movie and then he drove me home."

"Sure," Cameron elongated the word through a grin.

I rolled my eyes, and Nolan snorted. "Don't pay any attention to him, Zoey, he's just jealous."

Cameron exaggerated a laugh. "Oh please. We both know I can get any girl, or guy for that matter, that I want. That football player at the bar was practically drooling over me. *I* rejected *him*."

"Sure," I mocked, drawing out the word just as he had.

He moved to the hallway and set the tripod down so that the lens faced the bathroom door.

"C'mon ghost, show me how you slam the door," he said.

Nolan raised an eyebrow at him and then turned to me.

"How about a glass of wine while Cam talks to himself?" he joked.

I tried to hide a smile as I replied, "sure."

"When I'm on TV as a famous ghost hunter, you'll both be sorry you mocked me," Cameron sassed.

Nolan emerged from the kitchen soon after and handed a glass to me. Standing next to me, he leaned in, his eyes on Cameron's back. "How long before he gets bored with staring at the door?"

Cameron turned away from the camera to scowl at Nolan. "I heard that," he spat, sticking his tongue out.

"Let's go sit," Nolan gestured to the couch with his wineglass.

I followed him to the living room and sat beside him. He casually rested his arm across the back of the couch behind me, just far enough away that he wasn't touching me. We watched in amusement as Cameron attempted to film the ghost.

"What the heck man? Where is this ghost?" Cameron groaned.

"Maybe he went to get dinner," Nolan joked.

Cameron rolled his eyes. "Very funny."

"I've heard that ghosts can only be seen in night vision mode. Does your camera do infrared?" I asked.

He shook his head, and his face lit up with an idea. "I might be able to borrow an IR camera from the videography professor I had class with at Meridion College. I'll ask him tomorrow."

With that, he turned the camera off and deconstructed the tripod before joining us on the couch. "Movie?"

"Sure," I said, and Nolan reached for the remote on the coffee table. Before he could touch it, the remote moved across the glass, landing on the floor on the opposite side of the table.

"Are you serious?" Cameron snorted. "As soon as I turn the camera off, the ghost is going to show itself."

I laughed. "I guess the ghost is camera shy."

Nolan shook his head. "I just bumped it."

Cameron scoffed, "no you didn't. I was watching. Your hand didn't touch the remote."

Nolan looked at him through the side of his eye. "Whatever you say, dude." He stood to pick up the remote and selected a movie.

***

The following afternoon, Cameron arrived with the infrared camera and a digital recorder that he'd borrowed from the videography professor.

We waited until it was dark outside and played a game of cards while the devices recorded the hallway.

Nolan smiled as he set a final card on the table, winning the game. Cameron stood to inspect his footage. He lifted the camera and sighed, "oh, man."

"What's wrong?" I asked, placing a clip over the bag of chips in my hand.

"The battery drained," he replied, setting the camera back in his bag.

Nolan stood, and the light above us flickered. "I think the ghost is mocking you," he teased.

Cameron glared at the light, and I asked, "Aren't ghosts said to use batteries as energy?"

His face lit up. "You're right! I bet the ghost drained my battery."

"Or the camera is super old because the school hasn't bought any new ones since the 80s," Nolan suggested.

Cameron held up the digital recorder, choosing to ignore Nolan's jab. "This is still on, though. Maybe it captured something."

He hit play on the digital recorder, and we huddled together to listen. About ten minutes into the recording, we heard three distinct taps.

I gasped. "That sounded just like the tapping noises I heard in my apartment."

"Tapping in an apartment building," Noland repeated, "Definitely a ghost. Definitely not just someone else in the building tapping on something."

I glared at him. "Carter is the only other person in my building and he said he didn't do it. How do you explain that?"

"Maybe he lied," Nolan said with a shrug. "Look, I'm not saying you're wrong, I'm just saying it's not very solid proof of the paranormal."

Cameron's face lit up. "Maybe we can capture the same sound at Zoey's place."

***

Cameron drove the three of us to my apartment, where Carter stood on the patio drinking a beer. I smiled at him, and he cheered, "Hey, Zo, long time no see."

I unlocked the door to my apartment and looked back just in time to see Carter shoot a warning glare at Nolan.

"What's his problem?" Nolan asked, as I shut the door behind us.

Cameron chimed in. "He's just salty that Zoey has taste. He's been trying to get in her pants for months."

I sighed. "He doesn't actually want to be in a relationship with me, though. He just wants to check me off his bucket list."

"Sounds like a real nice guy," Nolan muttered sarcastically.

I felt a little bad for bashing Carter. He was, at least at some point, someone I considered a great friend.

I clarified, "he's not that bad. I just wish he'd accept the fact that I'm not interested."

"Why doesn't he just find some girl on campus? The university is full of girls that will sleep with anything that breathes." Nolan inquired.

"Because that would be too easy," I said, rolling my eyes in disgust.

"Anyway," I said, "let's see if we can catch this ghost."

Cameron set the digital recorder on the bathroom vanity.

"This is where she saw the girl in the mirror," he explained to Nolan.

I nodded to confirm, and Cameron pressed record. Then we stood in the doorway, unsure what to do next.

"Now what?" Nolan looked at the device.

I shrugged. "I can make popcorn."

"Works for me," Cameron agreed.

***

We finished our snack and returned to the bathroom to listen to the recording. Nolan's eyes went wide as three taps came through the device.

I looked around the bathroom and tapped on a few objects. Knocking my finger against the mirror, we froze. I tapped the mirror again.

"Holy crap, that's exactly what it sounded like," Cameron said.

I looked at the mirror and then back to Cameron. "You don't think it could be her, do you?"

His smile grew. "It's totally Martha trying to get our attention," he agreed.

"Hold on," Cameron pulled out his phone. "I have the recording from Nolan's house, too."

He played the recording and Cameron tapped on the mirror as the same sound came through his phone speaker.

Cameron smiled, looking up at Nolan. "Believe me now?"

Nolan nodded slowly, "it definitely sounds similar," he admitted.

Chapter 8

We spent the next few months attempting to make contact with the spirit, electing to spend most of our time at Nolan's apartment for the sake of avoiding Carter.

One sunny August day, Cameron suggested we sample a new restaurant downtown that had outdoor seating.

"Our manager, Tom, said it was really good," Cameron assured me.

"Okay," I replied with a shrug. "I'm always down for trying something new."

"I invited Nolan," Cameron said, "I figured we could talk about our next ghost hunt."

I nodded. "Sounds good."

Later that night, I entered the dimly lit restaurant and searched the room for my friend.

I looked around at the white table drapes and noticed Nolan sitting at a table in the center of the room.

As I sat down, I commented, "if I'd known it was this fancy, I would have dressed nicer."

He shrugged. "It's really not that fancy."

The host took our drink orders and poured us each a glass of chardonnay as we waited for Cameron.

Nolan took a sip and set his glass down. "So I was thinking..."

I used the pause to tease him. "I'm so proud of you. That's a big step."

"Funny," he laughed. "Sounds like you're spending too much time with Cam, he's rubbing off on you."

"You might be right about that," I agreed. "But anyway, what were you thinking about?"

Before he could answer, Cameron walked up behind me and placed his hands on my shoulders. "Boo!"

I jumped, nearly spilling my wine, and he laughed, as did Nolan.

We talked throughout dinner about how to make contact with the entity in Nolan's apartment.

I couldn't help but wonder what it was he'd wanted to say earlier. Whatever it was, it seemed he didn't want to say it in front of Cameron.

***

After dinner, Nolan and I returned to his apartment to watch a movie. As the film ended, he leaned down to rest his forehead against mine. His fingertips brushed my cheek as he softly tucked my hair behind my ear. I closed my eyes as our lips met and he adjusted himself to face me, deepening the connection. I rested a hand on his shoulder and wrapped the other around his neck, pulling him closer. He gently lowered my back to the couch cushion, refusing to break the kiss.

I wanted this more than I was willing to admit, even to myself. But I couldn't begin to think about being in a relationship right now.

I lightly pushed him back, so I could look at him and quickly thought of something to distract from our closeness.

"What did you want to tell me at the restaurant?" I asked.

Before he could reply, glass shattered in the bathroom, and I screamed in response. Nolan jumped off of me, assuming a defensive stance.

I stood behind him, gripping his bicep, in fear. "What was that?"

He shook his head, shaking free of my grip. "Wait here," he said.

I watched him move toward the kitchen and cautiously followed close behind him. I peaked over his shoulder into the bathroom. A soap dispenser slowly rolled back and forth on the tile floor as if it had just fallen. He leaned to pick it up and turned to face the mirror, which now donned a fresh crack as if something had hit it.

He stared at the crack, still holding the soap dispenser. "What the hell?"

***

We called Cameron, who eagerly agreed to tell Tom that he was feeling ill. Within twenty minutes, Cameron arrived with the infrared camera. He immediately got to work, setting up the camera in the bathroom. He turned the bathroom light off and shut the door, then suggested, "let's try the Ouija board again. Maybe that will encourage the ghost to show itself."

Cameron pulled the board from his backpack and the three of us sat around it on the living room floor.

I took a deep breath.

"Did you break the mirror?" I asked.

The light above us went out, and an eerie feeling swept through the room. We let our hands fall to our sides as the same light slowly brightened.

The planchet began to slide toward a letter, our hands nowhere near it. We watched as a phrase came through. S-T-A-Y-A-W-A-Y.

"What does that mean?" Cameron said, moving his eyes from mine to Nolan's.

The planchet moved again. N-O-C-O-N-T-A-C-T.

I furrowed my brow. "You don't want to talk to us?" I asked.

"You're talking to us now," Cameron scoffed.

The planchet moved once more.

G-I-R-L.

"What girl?" Nolan asked the empty room.

"Martha?" I whispered.

The game piece moved again, stopping on the word "goodbye."

Cameron stood and stomped to the bathroom in frustration. He removed the IR camera from the tripod and set the tripod on the dining room table before wedging himself between Nolan and I on the couch.

"Maybe I at least caught something on this," he said.

He navigated to the playback screen, and we watched the small display together. Just as we were starting to lose hope, a translucent ball of light appeared in front of the mirror and moved in a diagonal line toward the bathroom door. Cameron rushed to rewind the video, and we watched it again.

"That's an orb!" Cameron pointed at the ball of light.

"An orb?" Nolan raised an eyebrow.

Cameron shook his head, annoyed. "Don't you know anything? Ghosts show up as orbs when they're trying to manifest."

"So you caught a ghost on camera?" Nolan asked.

Cameron sighed, loudly. "No. I caught an orb."

"But something was trying to come through?" I clarified.

"Maybe," Cameron shrugged. He added, "glad I don't have to sleep with that ghost. It seemed grumpy."

I looked at Nolan for a reaction, and he glared at Cameron. "Gee, thanks dude."

Cameron threw up his hands in response and said, "Hey, it's not my fault the ghost in your apartment is a douche."

"I have a pullout couch if you want to stay at my place," I offered, looking across Cameron to meet Nolan's eyes.

Chapter 9

C arter was standing in his usual post-workout spot on the patio when we arrived at my apartment. He took a sip from his beer bottle as we approached my door. Swallowing the contents of the container he slurred, "she's only with you because she feels bad for you."

I glared at him. "I'm not *with* anyone."

Nolan puffed out his chest and spat back, "she's with me because I treat her like a person, not some prize to take home at the end of the night and show off to your friends."

"Nolan, please," I begged.

He lowered his gaze to me and let out a sharp breath eyeing Carter as he stepped inside my apartment.

Carter called after us, "you watch, the second you become old news, she'll come crawling right back to me, just like always."

I slammed the door in response and shook my head as I sighed. "He can be such an asshole sometimes."

Nolan walked to the kitchen and poured us each a glass of wine. He passed one to me as we relaxed into the couch cushions.

"What did he mean when he said you always crawl back to him?" Nolan asked.

I paused, trying to decide whether I wanted to answer. Finally, I revealed, "I've always had this kind of internal struggle when it comes to him."

"Meaning?" Nolan urged me to continue.

"We used to be really good friends, then we weren't friends at all for a while..." I trailed off.

"And now?" Nolan asked.

"Now, he seems to think I should just forget everything that's ever happened between us and give him another chance," I replied.

"Probably, because I always do give him another chance," I added.

"So you guys have dated in the past?" Nolan asked. "Is that why he's so volatile around me?"

"I have no interest in him," I clarified, "and no we never dated."

I set my glass on the table and pleaded, "Can we please talk about something else?"

"Sure," he agreed, "sorry I didn't mean to upset you."

"It's okay," I forgave him, then quickly thought of a new topic. "Do you think it could really be a ghost in your apartment...and mine for that matter?

He breathed. "I don't even know what to think anymore, to be honest."

I turned to him. "I mean. We both saw the planchet move by itself, right?"

He nodded.

"But maybe there was a breeze, or the floor wasn't level, right?" I asked, not sure who it was I was trying to convince.

"I'm sure there's some logical explanation," he replied, "Right?"

I searched the room for a response.

"I know what I saw that day in the mirror. It looked just like Martha Meridion," I said.

"Maybe the reflections are playing tricks on us," he offered.

I thought for a moment. "How do you explain your mirror breaking then?"

He shrugged, even the skeptic didn't seem to have an explanation for that.

We talked on the couch for a while longer until I started to get tired. "I'm going to go to bed."

Nolan nodded and I pointed to an ottoman in the corner as I told him, "there are extra blankets in there."

"Thanks," he replied.

***

I woke the next morning to the sound of my door creaking, and I lifted my chin to see Nolan peaking through the doorway.

"Good morning," he said quietly.

I smiled in response, laying my head back down.

As the sun peaked around the edges of my sage-colored curtains, I slid off the bed. I collected an outfit from my dresser and made my way to the bathroom to shower and change. When I stepped into the bathroom, Nolan was already sitting at the kitchen counter.

"I have to head to work, but I was thinking maybe this weekend we could go on a little trip together?" he said.

I shrugged, "I don't have any plans this weekend. What did you have in mind?"

He grinned proudly. "It's a surprise. But I think it could get us some answers," he explained.

I shot him a look of suspicion. "Okay. Is Cameron going?"

"I thought it'd be better if it was just the two of us," he said.

"This isn't a date," I said, and it was more of a question than a statement.

"Not a date," Nolan agreed.

***

Two days later, Nolan stopped by my apartment to pick me up. We were in the car for two hours before he finally announced, "we're almost there."

I began paying more attention to the surroundings in an attempt to guess where we were headed. The tree line along the side of the road became thicker and thicker until it was impossible to see through the forest. A cobblestone wall came into view, and my eyes followed it to a large stone sign that read, "Susquehanna State Asylum for the Insane."

"What are we doing here?" I inquired.

He parked the car in a small lot outside the main building of the hospital and replied, "I booked a tour for us. I was talking to my students about Meridion Manor and one of them mentioned that they went on a tour of the asylum and the tour guide told them a story about Martha."

I looked up at the massive yellow-brick structure. A rusting clock tower rose above the twin rectangular structures on either side of it, dwarfing the main entrance that sat between them. Two wooden doors stood tucked behind the bricks, coating them in darkness. I stepped out of the car and scanned the building as we approached. Lines of windows extended as far as the eye could see on either side of the main building. Additional buildings stood either side of it. We came upon an empty white foundation covered in algae and I studied the cracks in the old stone as we walked past it.

We stopped at the foot of the steps, the history of the location hovering over us like a grey cloud.

Nolan broke the silence. "This place is definitely creepy."

I nodded as he pulled one of the entrance doors open and held it for me. "Ladies first," he said.

I stepped through the door into the castle-like atrium that smelled of mildew. The ceiling towered above us, the white paint chipping away in spots, revealing bare rock behind it. Staircases covered in cracked and missing tiles led to the balconies above. Pieces of metal banister hung from the third floor, threatening to fall at any minute.

"Be right with you." A sing-song male voice echoed off the walls.

We continued to take in our surroundings as we waited for the guide to join us. Not long after a man emerged from one of the metal doors to the left of us. He wore white-washed jeans, trendy sneakers and a floral, short-sleeve blouse with flowy chiffon sleeves. He walked with a swagger and paused in front of us, flicking his dark brown hair out of his eyes with a twitch of his head.

"Here for the tour?" he asked.

"Yeah, Nolan and Zoey," Nolan confirmed, pointing to me with his thumb.

"Amazing," he clasped his hand together, "I'm Jaime, I'll be your tour guide."

We nodded acknowledging him and he continued, "Have you guys been here before?"

We both shook our heads, and he smiled. "Amazing," he repeated. "What brings you here? Date night?"

"Oh, no, we're not," I replied.

I looked at Nolan to answer and he said, "we went to Meridion Manor a while ago and we heard that there was a connection between the manor and this asylum."

Jaime's eyes lit up. "Oh, yes," he nodded. "Edith Meridion was a patient here when she died in 1906. That was the same year the asylum shut down, fun fact."

"Edith Meridion is Martha's mother?" I clarified.

"Yes," Jaime confirmed. "Formerly, Edith Sullivan. She was Landon Meridion's wife."

Motioning for us to follow Jaime led us up the staircase to the right.

"We of course don't have time to see all 352,000 square feet of the complex, so we'll focus on the west wing, that's where Edith's room is," he explained.

He pointed to a portion of the loose banister. "Careful, the building is still under restoration. It was abandoned for a long time before the historical society purchased the land in 2004, so we still have a lot of work to do."

Tile crunched below us as we followed Jaime to the fourth floor. He paused at the top of the staircase to wait for us. "Welcome to the west wing," he said as we stepped into the hallway.

The long, straight hallway complimented the atrium with peeling white paint and debris scattering the floor. As we walked past the rooms lining either side, Nolan and I peaked in to see broken wire beds and spray-painted walls.

"The asylum had some issues with vandalism in the 80s, but the building is locked now anytime tours aren't taking place," Jaime explained.

A breeze came in through an open window on the right side of the hallway as we passed by and the smell of mildew filled my nostrils, causing me to sneeze.

Jaime turned, "the dust can be pretty intense in here, that's why we leave the windows open."

Jaime stopped three doors from the end of the hallway and focused his attention on the doorway to our left. The three of us huddled in the area where a door should've been.

"This was Edith Meridion's room," Jaime said, stepping toward the center of the room.

He gestured for us to join him and said, "you'll notice this is one of the few rooms in the hall not in shambles. The historical society used funding from the annual Halloween party last year to complete the restoration of Edith's room. The walls were stripped and repainted, the floors redone, and the furniture was created by a local craftsman. We even had the windows replaced with authentic Victorian glass."

He stepped back, leaning against a wall, giving us time to take in the room. A metal-framed hospital bed covered in fresh wool linens sat under a window at the back of the room. Next to it was a small, blue side table with a drinking glass on top, and on the wall to our left, hung a mirror, nearly identical to the one we'd seen in Martha's bedroom at the manor.

I stepped toward the mirror for a closer look. "Did this mirror come from Martha's room?"

Jaime nodded, pushing away from the wall and stepping toward me. "Good question. No, it's actually a different mirror," he replied. "Edith and Loretta Meridion believed that you could speak to spirits through mirrors. So when Perida, Edith's niece, came to visit her in the asylum, Edith begged her to have this mirror created so that she could speak to her sister."

I looked at Nolan whose eyes met mine as if we were sharing the same thought.

Jaime continued. "Landon Meridion had Edith admitted to the asylum after the disappearance of her brother-in-law. Landon claimed that Edith was speaking to a ghost in the manor. She reported hearing noises, books moving on their own, cold breezes coming out of nowhere, etc."

I looked at Nolan and wondered if, like me, he was thinking about the book that had moved during the Valentine's Day party.

Jaime continued, "Landon feared she'd gone insane, so he contacted the asylum and they brought her here for treatment."

Jaime's face looked sad as he added, "unfortunately, the asylum was not known for successful treatments. She later died right here in this room."

The silence that followed gave dramatic effect to his last statement. He moved toward the door and said, "which brings us to our next stop on the tour. Follow me."

I turned to Nolan and whispered, "we saw a book move in the manor."

He nodded, still processing what we were being told, we followed Jaime into the room across the hall.

Jaime gestured toward a metal chair with ripped aquamarine upholstery in the center of the room. It looked like something you'd see in a dentist's office.

"This is the lobotomy room," Jaime explained.

I flinched in disgust at the thought as he continued, "unfortunately these procedures were very common at the asylum, and Edith's case was no different. Doctors performed a lobotomy on March 11, 1906 in an attempt to rid her of the demons they believed were causing her to see ghosts. She died just an hour later from complications."

"That's so sad," I whispered.

Jaime nodded in agreement. "Edith's story has always upset me. She deserved so much better."

Nolan chimed in. "Landon Meridion was responsible for his brother's death, right?"

Jaime nodded solemnly. "That's what many believe, yes. A few years ago while they were working to restore the manor, they did take up the floorboards of Edith's library. It was believed that he'd hidden the body there during the construction of the shelves. Nothing was found though."

He looked at each of us and whispered, "between the three of us, I've always believed that Edith really was communicating with spirits."

"Have you heard of any ghost sightings at the manor, other than what Edith supposedly saw?" I asked him.

He shook his head. "I've heard that a few guests claimed to have been attacked by the ghost of Landon Meridion. He's said to be very protective of Martha," Jaime replied.

"Interesting," I said, nodding. "What do you mean by attacked?"

He replied, "oh, you know, like lights shattering and objects being thrown. Stuff like that."

I looked at Nolan. Was it possible that Landon, rather than Martha, had followed us home after the Halloween party?"

***

Once the tour concluded, Nolan drove me back to my apartment. I turned to face him and said, "I had a great time today, thank you."

He smiled in response and asked, "I'll see you for pizza on Friday?"

I nodded and exited the car making my way to the porch where Carter was standing amongst dozens of empty beer bottles which were littering the patio.

I acknowledged his presence with a look and he stepped in front of me blocking the path to my door.

"You sure move on fast don't you?" he spat.

"What are you talking about?" I tried to walk around him, but failed.

He sneered, "don't act like I didn't just see you practically drooling over him."

"What are you talking about?" I retorted.

As I once again tried to move past him, he gripped my shoulders and spun around so that my back was against the exterior of the building.

I protested, "let go of me."

His nose nearly touching mine, I stared into his dilated pupils as he slurred, "I want to know why you think he's better than me."

"Carter stop," I tried to shove him off, but it was no use, I added, "How many times do I have to tell you? I'm not interested."

"What does he have that I don't?" he spat, the smell of alcohol filling the air as he spoke into my nose."

He leaned in to kiss me, and I turned my head to avoid him.

"Get off of me." I shouted, attempting to shove him once more.

A car door slammed in the parking lot and I could hear gravel kicking up as someone quickly approached. Carter was thrown to the ground moments later. I hardly had time to register what was happening before Nolan knelt to the ground, one hand gripping the front of Carter's shirt and the other in a fist ready to swing.

"You ever think of touching her again, I will rip you apart with my bare hands!" Nolan growled.

I couldn't decide if I was horrified by his actions or turned on by them. Maybe a bit of both.

Nolan pushed off Carter's chest and stood to face me. His expression softened as he placed his hands gently on my cheeks. "Are you hurt?"

I shook my head and let out the breath I'd been holding. He wrapped an arm around me and led me to the door.

I fumbled with my keys and tried to unlock the door. Nolan gently worked the key from my hand and let us in.

"You're okay now. I won't let him hurt you," he promised.

A single tear rolled down my face as I took a deep breath. Even on the worst day of high school, Carter had never acted like that.

I sat on the couch, my head in my hands and tried to combat the tears threatening to fall. Nolan sat beside me, draping an arm over my shoulder and pulled me into him. I turned to bury my face in his shoulder and he held me as I cried.

When I finally managed to calm down, Nolan suggested, "you should call the police. His behavior needs to be reported."

I leaned away from his chest so I could look at him, and replied, "he just had an off night. I'd rather just forget about it."

He scoffed, "you can't just let him get away with it, Zoey."

"He's my friend, Nolan," I turned from the stove to look at him. "After how much he's done for me, I can't do that to him."

"What has he done for you, other than harass you?" Nolan interrogated me.

"He drives me around all the time," I reminded him.

"I can drive you anywhere you need to go," he quickly replied. "You don't need him."

"Nolan, stop," I pleaded, "he didn't hurt me. Please, let's just forget about it."

"Fine. Will you at least stay at my place tonight?" he asked, "just to give him time to calm down."

I breathed, "if that'll make you feel better, fine."

Staring into his eyes I affirmed, "but I'm not sleeping with you."

***

I awoke, startled in the middle of the night. My heart was pounding, I was certain someone was in the house with us. I slipped out of bed and peaked into the living room where Nolan was still sound asleep on the couch.

"Nolan," I hissed, over and over until he finally stirred.

"What?" he groggily replied.

"Someone is in the kitchen," I whispered.

"What?" he said again.

"I heard someone talking," I clarified.

He propped himself up on his elbows and sleepily replied, "it's probably just one of the neighbors talking to someone."

I nodded, but I wasn't convinced. Nolan raised an eyebrow as I continued to stand in front of him, unsure how to ask for what I wanted.

"Are you okay?" he finally asked.

I took a deep breath. "Will you come to sleep next to me?" I said shyly.

He laughed. "Sure," he said, then mockingly added, "I thought you weren't sleeping with me?"

I glared at him. "You know damn well what I meant, and it's still not happening," I retorted.

Nolan joined me in his room and shut the door before laying down beside me.

Moments later, a muffled voice sounded just outside his bedroom door, and the knob wiggled. Nolan shot out from under the covers and lunged for the door. I pulled the blankets up to my chin in fear as he flung the door open. I remained in the bed, but lifted my chin to see over Nolan's shoulder as he peered down the hallway. He stormed out of the room, checking the apartment for any sign of an intruder. When he returned to the doorway, his limbs were frozen in a protective stance. Full of adrenaline, he shakily whispered, "there's no one here." It seemed like he was trying to convince himself as he said it.

An unsettling feeling fell over me and I felt my breath catch in my throat. I stared into his eyes, a look of concern on my face.

I swallowed. "You heard it too though?"

He nodded slowly, returning to the bed and slid in next to me.

I whispered, "it had to have been the wind. Right?"

"Yeah," he replied, but there was something in his voice that told me he wasn't convinced. Relaxing into the mattress he pulled me into his chest and we struggled to fall back asleep.

Chapter 10

The following day, after work, I packed a duffle bag of clothes and essentials. I'd decided it would be best to spend a few days with Nolan, just long enough to diffuse the tension with Carter. I listened for the sound of Carter's weight set hitting the floor, and when I was sure he was busy with a workout, I texted Nolan and watched out the window for his car. As soon as Nolan pulled into the parking lot, I cracked my front door open just enough to peek out and ensure Carter wasn't on the porch. I quickly locked the door behind me and jogged through the rain, opening the back door of his car to deposit my bag before sliding into the front seat. I took one last glance at the empty patio as Nolan placed his hands on the gear stick.

"Ready to go?" He asked.

"Yeah," I nodded with a smile, breathing out a sigh of relief.

***

We pulled into the parking lot of Nolan's building and he quickly exited the vehicle, grabbing my bag from the backseat before I had a chance to. He carried it to the front door, which he held open for me, and I smiled as I stepped inside.

The smell of tomato sauce and oregano filled the room. Two plates, accompanied by two glasses of red wine, had been thoughtfully set on the tablecloth atop the table. I looked at Nolan, who grinned. "I made us spaghetti," he said.

He led me to the table where we sat across from each other. Explaining his reason for the meal, he added, "I thought you could use a relaxing dinner after what happened last night."

"Thank you," I said, looking down at my hand as I fidgeted with my fork.

"Is everything okay?" He asked, concerned.

"Yeah," I sighed. "It's just that... I still can't believe Carter did that. He's never acted like that before."

I could tell Nolan was uncomfortable and didn't know what to say. To be fair, I wasn't sure I wanted him to say anything, anyway. I decided it was best to change the subject.

"How was school today?" I asked.

He breathed, relieved at the change of topic. "It was interesting, to say the least," he replied.

I raised an eyebrow, intrigued.

"One of my students in second period thought it would be funny to unplug the power strip that powers all of the desktops in my classroom," he began. "Long story short, it took me almost the entire period to figure out why the computers weren't working."

He took a bite of pasta before continuing. "So now we're behind an entire day of lessons, all because some little brat unplugged a power strip."

I smirked. "You have to admit, it is a little funny."

"Now it is," he agreed. "At the time, it wasn't funny at all."

I swirled the spaghetti around my fork and took a bite, washing it down with a sip of wine.

Nolan gestured to me with his fork. "What about you? How was the restaurant?"

I shrugged. "Cameron hit on a bunch of young girls. I got hit on by a bunch of old men. Same as always."

Nolan shook his head with a chuckle. "Gotta love Cam."

I thought for a moment. This moment of silence was as good a time as any to bring up what I really wanted to talk about.

"The tour guide at the asylum mentioned that spirits can talk through mirrors," I said. "Do you think that's what Martha is doing?"

He shrugged. "Why would she want to contact us?"

"I don't know," I admitted. "But there must be some reason all of this stuff keeps happening to us."

"She hasn't come to my mirror, just yours," Nolan pointed out.

"Your mirror cracked the other day," I reminded him, adding, "maybe we can ask her."

"Ask her what?" Nolan swallowed a sip of wine.

"What she wants," I said, as if it should've been obvious.

"So, your plan is to talk to a mirror?" Nolan eyed me skeptically.

I exhaled. "Okay, it sounds insane when you say it like that?"

He shrugged with a playful smile. "Maybe you are crazy."

I playfully shoved his shoulder and slowly allowed my expression to become serious once again. "Honestly, though, I know what I saw that day, and we both saw that planchet move by itself. We both heard something in your apartment, too. You can't deny that something strange is going on, even if there is a logical explanation."

He nodded. "I'll give you that. There have definitely been some, shall we say, unusual events lately."

I stood from the couch. "So, it doesn't hurt to try contacting her, right? If nothing happens and we look crazy, then we can just keep it between us and pretend it never happened."

He nodded and moved to rise from the couch, falling backward as if something had shoved him. I gulped down my fear and turned to meet his wide eyes. He allowed a deep breath to escape his lungs before he spoke.

"What the hell was that?" he asked me.

The lights in the bathroom went out, followed by the hallway lights, then the kitchen and dining room went dark.

We slowly angled our heads upward toward the last light in the apartment, just in time to watch it explode with a pop.

Shards of glass rained down to the carpet and Nolan shielded my body with his, hiding his face in my hair. I gripped his t-shirt, my face tucked into his chest. Our heartbeats picked up.

My stomach dropped as the feeling of being watched crept into my soul, just as it had the other nights I believed

I'd encountered spirits. Nolan lifted his head and began to shake. His breathing grew more and more unsteady. I hesitantly rotated my neck, my head never leaving the comfort of his chest. My jaw fell open in horror as my eyes landed on the figure towering above us.

My fist tightened against Nolan's shirt as we stared at the dark, shadow-like mass. You could barely make out what looked like arms and legs through the swirling black cloud. The eyes, on the other hand, there was no mistaking the eyes. Two yellow almond-shaped lights glowed from its head like a lighthouse beckoning a ship's crew to a watery grave. Its mouth, a dark void just below its eyes, fell open and it let out a breath that howled through the room like the wind on a cool fall night.

Our eyes followed the figure's as it slowly rose from the floor and hovered above us. Nolan pinned his back against the couch, pulling me closer. We were both speechless.

"The girl is mine," it said in a low tone, its expression impossible to discern.

Nolan held me tighter and bravely replied, "don't touch her."

Our wine glasses on the coffee table lifted and the figure's eyes moved to the right as the glasses hung in front of our faces. The figure's eyes burned into mine as the glasses repelled from each other, slamming into the walls to the left and right of us, shattering.

The figure righted its head and spoke once more, "stay away."

With that, the figure was gone.

We clung to each other for some time, unable to move or speak.

Finally, Nolan's biceps relaxed, and he asked, "You saw it too?"

I nodded, still staring at the spot where the figure had been. Shakily, I replied. "What was that thing?"

He breathed. "I don't know, but it certainly wasn't Martha."

***

Nolan and I remained on the couch until morning, both too scared to move. I awoke with my head on his chest.

He groggily looked down at me and said, "please tell me that it was all a dream?"

I sucked in a breath as I shook my head. "It was real."

I rose from his chest, tucking my legs beneath me.

What do we do?" Nolan asked.

There was only one thing I could think to do to confirm what we'd both seen. I replied, "we call Cameron."

***

Cameron let himself into the apartment, discarding his jacket on the floor just inside the door as I finished cleaning up the shattered lightbulb from the night before.

"So wait. You guys actually saw a ghost? Like a real ghost?" Cameron inquired.

We nodded and he continued, "this is insane. What did it look like? What did it say? Did it..."

I held up a hand to stop him as I discarded the contents of the dustpan into the kitchen trash. "Whoa, one question at a time," I said.

Cameron took a breath, dramatically fanning his face to show he was calming down.

"Where was it?" Cameron asked.

Nolan pointed to the living room. "Right in front of the couch," he answered, adding, "I still can't believe it."

Cameron moved toward the couch and stood in front of the coffee table, turning to us. "Here?"

I nodded. "It was like a talking shadow. You should've seen its eyes," I explained, "it was like two flashlights staring into your soul."

He looked around the area as if he was going to find something and spotted the broken wine glasses on the other side of the room.

"What happened here?" he asked.

"Dang, I thought I got it all," I replied, picking up the dustpan.

I turned and stared at the wall Cameron had pointed to. The sound of shattering glass played through my mind.

I took a breath before explaining, "the shadow flung our wine glasses across the room. It was weird, it was like he was trying to make a point. But neither of us can figure out what the point was."

"Interesting," Cameron replied with a nod. "Did it say anything?"

I looked at Nolan, and he stood to put an arm around me. "It said that it wants Zoey."

Cameron's eyes went wide and his mouth fell open. "No way! Do you guys know what this means?"

With raised eyebrows, we waited for him to continue.

He snorted at our lack of enthusiasm. "Zoey, we can use you as bait to contact it!"

Taken aback, I paused and spoke to Nolan, "it didn't exactly say it wants me," I clarified. It said, "the girl is mine."

I turned to Cameron and added, "and it also told us to stay away. I don't think it wants to be contacted."

He thought for a moment and shrugged. "Did it say anything about filming it?"

Nolan and I looked at each other, and Cameron scurried to the front door to retrieve his night vision camera. He set up a tripod near the front door so that it faced the couch, the bathroom visible in the background.

"From this angle, I should be able to see if anything happens in the living room, kitchen or hallway," he explained.

After hitting the record button, he returned to his backpack and removed the Ouija board. Holding it up, he smiled manically. "I think it's time to get some answers."

I sighed. "Cam, I just said it doesn't want to be contacted."

He scoffed, "well then, it shouldn't have messed with my friends."

Nolan and I shook our heads and reluctantly moved to the living room, as Cameron set the board on the coffee table. Kneeling on the carpet, we each placed a finger on the planchet and Cameron spoke, "Who are you?"

We exchanged glances as we waited for the planchet to move.

When it didn't, Nolan asked, "Why are you here?"

I think Cameron and I were both a little surprised at his willingness to participate.

The planchet remained still.

I looked at the ceiling. "What do you want with me?"

The planchet began to glide across the board and we watched as it spelled out, M-A-R-T-H-A. Nolan and I locked eyes, breathing heavily, and I added. "Martha, is it you that we're speaking to?"

The planchet moved to the word "no."

"Who are we speaking to, then?" Cameron asked.

Once more, the planchet slid across the board under our fingers, "S-T-A-Y-A-W-A-Y.

Cameron grunted in frustration. "Why do you only show yourself when I'm not around?"

A long beep sounded from the front door, and Cameron's head snapped toward the sound. He jumped to his feet and hurried toward the camera. Leaning down to the display screen, his face fell. "The battery died."

"You didn't charge it before you came?" Nolan teased him.

Cameron peaked around the camera to glare at him as he said, "it was fully charged, thank you very much. If you knew anything about ghosts, you would know they drain batteries."

Nolan gave me a look as if to say, "Can you believe this guy?"

I shrugged. "That is what they say on all the ghost hunting shows."

Cameron grinned and spoke excitedly, "I can't believe a ghost just drained my battery. I feel like a certified ghost hunter now."

I looked down at the Ouija board and placed my index finger back on the game piece.

"Did you do that?" I asked.

The planchet wiggled, like it was trying to move, and then stilled. I pulled my hand away in defeat and watched as it slid just a smidge before flying across the room as if someone had thrown it. The planchet bounced off the wall and landed on the carpet.

Cameron locked eyes with me and ran to retrieve it before returning to the board. He set the planchet in the center and we all jumped at a thud that came from the front door. We looked up from the board to see Cameron's tripod tipped onto its side.

The bathroom door slammed shut, and we rushed to it. Nolan reached for the knob as I clung to his arm and Cameron clung to mine. He twisted the handle and let the door fall open. We gasped at the message written in soap on the mirror, "leave."

The faucet turned on and the handle began to spin on its own until it broke free from the counter. It flew to the ceiling, followed by a geyser of water that sprayed the mirror. The soap message bubbled into suds and seeped down the mirror, disappearing.

We stood in the hallway, staring at the mirror in disbelief. Suddenly, Nolan freed his arm from my grip, and lunged toward the bathroom vanity. He collected as many towels as he could, throwing them on top of the counter before turning the water line off below. The gush of water ceased.

Cameron and I rushed into the bathroom, taking a towel in each hand, and began sopping up the water. Once we had soaked up most of it, Nolan knelt on the shag rug and laughed out of disbelief.

"How am I going to explain this to my landlord?" he asked himself.

Chapter 11

I set down my fork, my mind weighing on the idea I'd wanted to bring up from the start of our meal. When I couldn't take it anymore, I finally said, "Nolan, I think we should go back to the Meridion Manor."

"I thought we agreed we were staying away like the ghost asked?" he sighed.

I exhaled. "What if it's trying to warn us about something?"

He slammed his fork onto his plate in frustration.

"What could it possibly be trying to warn us about Zoey? This is ridiculous."

I flinched at his words. I'd never seen him upset with me.

"I...I don't know," I stammered, "but it must want something if it keeps contacting us. My bathroom lights are flickering on a daily basis now. And how many light bulbs have you replaced this week?"

He scoffed, "it very clearly told us to leave it alone, Zoey."

I stood, pushing my chair against the table in anger. "Then why does it keep contacting us?"

"How should I know?" he spat, standing to shove his chair the same way I had.

I sobbed. "I just want to try once, see if she'll appear in the mirror at the manor."

"No," Nolan barked. "I'm done."

My stomach dropped. We'd just started spending more time together. Should I have stuck with my instincts and hidden my feels better?

"Done with what, exactly?" I barked.

"All of it. This whole ghost thing has been nothing but problems," he huffed. "You won't shut up about it. Cameron won't shut up about it. I'm done with it," he ranted.

My lips trembled as a tear escaped my eye and rolled down my cheek. Just as I suspected, getting involved with a guy was a bad idea. Jokes on me for thinking he was different.

I turned to the door, stopping with my hand on the knob.

"Fine. I guess I'll shut up then," I said, and with that, I opened the door, stepped out and slammed it behind me.

I half expected, or maybe hoped, he would follow me into the parking lot. When he didn't, I knew it was over.

I tried to push the thought of him away as I walked along the sidewalk toward my apartment. But as I focused on the reds, oranges, and yellows of the leaves ready to fall, I wondered, *how can he still be in denial after what we saw?*

A tear rolled down my face at the thought. I had strong feelings for Nolan, feelings I wasn't even entirely ready to admit to myself. The thought of never seeing him again pained me in a way I didn't know was possible. Hell, I hadn't ever had a boyfriend, unless I counted Carter and I's elementary school fling.

My throat tightened, my eyes swelled, and the simple thought of eating something when I got home made me want to vomit.

After walking over two miles, I finally stepped onto the familiar gravel that blanketed my building's parking lot. I looked at the patio, hoping to see Carter standing there. Someone to talk to would've been nice, but the porch was empty and dark. I sighed and continued to my door, placing the key into the slot and turning it. I opened the door and once inside, I leaned back against it until the latch clicked closed. I closed my eyes and allowed a labored breath to escape my lips, then sucked in another, pushing off the door and making my way toward the bathroom.

I stepped into the bathroom and leaned against the grey vanity, supporting myself with both hands. Studying my reflection in the mirror, I turned the cold water on and let it run for a moment. Leaning down to splash water on my face in an attempt to subdue the swelling around my eyes, I sighed. My eyes still closed, I reached for the hand towel to my right and gently dabbed the water away from my face. Then, I set the towel on the countertop and returned my gaze to the mirror, stepping back in surprise at the pale freckled face staring back at me.

There was no mistaking her. Her jet black hair hung just below her breasts and the nightgown she wore was clearly not of this century.

"Martha?" I whispered, a chill running up my arms.

She nodded, her face emotionless.

My hands shaking, I asked for the answer I'd been craving for months, "What do you want from me?"

Her mouth unmoving, she placed her index finger to her lips and shook her head.

"You can't talk?" I guessed.

She nodded and pointed toward the hallway. I stepped into the doorway just in time to watch a picture frame fly out of my bedroom and land on the cream carpet of the hallway.

I approached the frame and leaned down to retrieve it, flipping it over in my hands. The maple frame had a leafy design. I ran my hands over it as my face dropped at the sight of the photo. It was the selfie Nolan and I had taken at the manor on Valentine's Day.

I reminisced for a moment and then returned to the mirror with the frame in hand. Martha was still there.

I held up the frame. "You saw us in the mirror, didn't you?"

Again, she just nodded.

There were so many questions I wanted to ask her. I finally said, "I don't know what you want from me."

She pointed to the picture frame in my hands, and I held it up. "Nolan?"

Her lips curled into a satisfied smile and she pointed to me, then lifted her other hand toward the frame. She brought her index fingers together in a line parallel to the countertop.

I furrowed my brows in confusion, letting my eyes explore the bathroom as I tried to decipher her actions.

I looked at the photo of Nolan and I, then I looked back at Martha.

"We're not together," I confirmed, mostly to her, but also to myself.

She shook her head and again touched her fingers together.

"You want us to get together?" I asked, confused.

She smiled in response.

"Why do you care if we're together or not?" I wondered.

Instead of replying, she disappeared.

Steadying my breathing, I tried to decide if what just happened had been real or another hallucination. I slowly made my way to the couch and lazily plopped down, setting the picture frame on the cushion beside me.

I started to cry.

Why am I incapable of being in a relationship? I wondered as tears cascaded down my cheeks.

I looked down at the photo and picked it up. Anger flooding through my veins, all at once I stood and flung the frame across the living room and grunted as it shattered against the wall that sat between mine and Carter's apartments.

***

I walked to the kitchen and poured a glass of wine. As I leaned against the counter, I lifted the glass to my lips and took a sip, savoring the sweet taste and the soft sting of the alcohol. I breathed out a relaxing sigh and wondered what to do next.

A frantic knock at the front door pulled me from my thoughts, and I set the glass on the countertop as I walked to the front door. I figured it must be Carter coming to inquire about the thud that the picture frame had caused. Bracing myself for the conversation, I fumbled with the deadbolt, and the knocking ceased only when I turned the knob.

Nolan stood just outside my door, tears in his eyes. Without waiting for an invitation, he stepped inside and wrapped his arms around me, pulling me close. He let our connection linger as tears fell down his cheeks.

"I'm sorry," he managed to whisper.

I failed to hold back my own tears. "Me too," I whimpered.

He held me for a few moments more and then pulled away, his hands on my shoulders.

Wiping his face with one hand, he said, "you're never going to believe what happened when you left."

I thought about Martha and the events that had unfolded during the last hour. "I wouldn't be so sure about that," I replied.

We walked to the kitchen, and I poured a glass of wine for Nolan. Then we sat on the kitchen bar stools. He took a large gulp from his glass and set it down, fidgeting with it.

"After you slammed the door..." he hesitated before continuing. "After you left the lights, they went crazy."

I could tell he was still struggling to believe his own story as his breath shook. "Zo, the bathroom lights wouldn't stop flickering, and then the water in the shower turned on," he explained. "The lights in the hallway turned on one by one, moving toward the bathroom." He kept spewing words. "I finally got up to look and there she was."

He paused, and I inferred, "Martha?"

He nodded. "She was...it was...it was her...in... my mirror." He let out a sob. "She wrote on the mirror in soap. I watched her draw the words, Zoey."

Nolan studied my face, trying to decide if I believed him. He should've known by now that I did.

"What did she write?" I asked.

He let out a breath. "Go."

I looked into his eyes as he added, "I knew. Don't ask me how I did, but I just knew she was telling me to go to you."

A tear rolled down my face, and I held back a sob as I brought my hand to his cheek.

"She came to me too," I revealed.

"What did she say?" he asked.

I shook my head, lowering my hand.

"She didn't say anything. It was like she was afraid to talk, or maybe she can't talk. I don't know, but she made it clear that she wanted us to be together."

"How?" He asked.

I pointed toward the floor where the shattered remnants of our selfie lay scattered across the carpet.

"That picture of us from the manor," I explained, "she threw it into the hallway while I was standing in the bathroom. I asked her if she wanted us to get back together and she nodded and then disappeared."

He sighed and lowered his gaze in thought.

"Why does a ghost care if we're together?" he asked.

I shrugged, wondering the same thing. "I have no idea," I whispered.

Our lips connected, and he pulled me close to him, lifting me from the chair as he stood. My hands in his hair, he slid the barstools out of the way with his foot and guided us toward my room.

***

I opened my eyes as the morning sun beamed through the curtains I'd unintentionally left open. Rubbing my eyes, I rolled over to find Nolan scrolling on his phone.

"Good morning," he said with a smile, lifting his arm as an invitation for me to cuddle into his chest.

I let out a relaxed sigh as I moved closer, placing my hand on his bare chest.

"This is nice," I said.

He reached for my chin and tilted my head toward his lips. Then, he kissed me softly and pulled away to apologize, "I'm sorry about last night. You're right, we need to get answers somehow. I think we should go to Meridion Manor, like you said. It's our best shot at getting answers."

I reached my arm across his torso and hugged him. "I think that's a great idea."

After snuggling for a bit longer, we got dressed, and I made breakfast. Then Nolan drove us to the manor.

As Nolan drove, I asked, "Do you think we should tell Cameron?"

Nolan shrugged. "Why would we?"

"It just feels like we're leaving him out. He was really excited about all the ghost stuff," I explained.

"You're right. Let's give him a call," Nolan replied, reaching for the AI assistant button on his dashboard.

"Call Cam," Nolan instructed.

"Thank you for calling Cam's Crack House. How can I help you?" Cameron laughed into the speaker.

Nolan chuckled, "grow up."

"Never," Cameron replied, "What's up?"

"Are you busy?" Nolan asked.

"I'm always available for you, sweety," Cameron cooed.

I giggled, "back off, he's taken."

"Oh, since when?" Cameron inquired.

"Can you be serious for five seconds Cam? We need to tell you something important," Nolan said sternly.

"Watch out, Zo, the conversation cop is here," Cameron teased.

Nolan sighed and chose to move on, "long story short, we're going to Meridion Manor to find out more about the ghost in my apartment. Do you want to come or not?"

"Hell yeah!" Cameron exclaimed, "when?"

"Now," I replied.

***

We met Cameron on the front porch of the manor and he immediately started questioning us. "You saw the shadow ghost again?"

Nolan and I exchanged glances. I wasn't sure how much I wanted Cameron to know about what had transpired the night before.

"We both saw Martha this time," I said.

Cameron's eyes went wide. "No way! What did she say?" he asked.

I looked at Nolan, who shrugged. "She said she wants us to be together, but we don't know why."

I chimed in, "we're hoping Ellie knows something that can help us figure out what she wants."

Cameron grabbed the door handle and opened it. "Well, then, what are we standing here for? Let's go," he said.

We entered the main hall of the manor and found Ellie hanging a portrait halfway up the staircase.

"It's so nice to see you again," she gleamed. "Zoey, right?"

I nodded with a smile. "This is Nolan and Cameron," I said, pointing to each of them.

"Hi, guys," she cheerily greeted them, wiping the dust from her hands onto her blue capris. She looked at each of us with a smile.

"What can I do for you guys?" she asked.

"This is going to sound insane," I admitted, looking at Nolan and Cameron for support. I let out a sigh. *Here goes nothing.*

"We think Martha is haunting us and we're hoping you might be able to help us figure out why," I spewed.

"Interesting," she paused. "What makes you think she's haunting you?"

Cameron, unable to hold in his excitement any longer, jumped in. "They've seen her in the mirror."

"The mirror upstairs?" Ellie clarified, pointing toward the second floor.

I shook my head. "My bathroom mirror," I paused before pointing to Nolan. "His too."

Before she had a chance to respond, I spoke again, "Is there anything you can tell us about the mirror that might explain why she's reaching out to us?"

She paused, taking in the minimal information we'd given her.

"Come with me," she said, turning to climb the stairs.

I looked at Cameron and Nolan, then shrugged and followed Ellie up the stairs. She led us to the familiar mint green room and stopped in front of the mirror.

She began to explain, "Martha's uncle, Reginald and Bauer, gifted her this mirror..."

Nolan cut her off, "What did you say his last name was?"

Ellie smiled and repeated herself, "Bauer."

"My last name is Bauer." Nolan stated, interrupting her again.

Ellie's eyes lit up. "The Bauer's were a local family, maybe you're related. We can check public records to find out."

Cameron gasped in excitement. "Maybe that's why Martha is trying to contact you! Maybe she thinks you're her uncle."

Nolan snorted. "I feel like I'd know if I was related to a murder victim."

Ellie commented, "such a sad story." She looked into the mirror. "I've always felt for Martha. Poor thing."

I thought about what Jaime told us at the asylum, and asked, "Have you ever heard about Martha communicating with people through the mirror?"

She nodded again. "The Meridion women believed that spirits could be contacted through mirrors. According to her diary, she learned this from a psychic named Perida."

My eyes grew. "As in, the Lady Perida that has the shop downtown?"

Cameron commented, "I don't think Lady Perida is *that* old."

Ellie giggled, "Lady Perida's shop, and name, have been passed down for many generations. It would likely have been her grandmother."

I looked at my friends. "Maybe it's time to pay Lady Perida another visit," I suggested.

They nodded and Cameron addressed Ellie, "Has Lady Perida ever done a reading on the manor?"

Her face went flat. "Once," she said, "since then, she won't step foot in the manor."

The three of us exchanged glances with each other, then I looked at Ellie and asked, "Why?"

She shrugged. "She would never say anything other than that there is something very dark connected to the place."

Cameron looked at the mirror. "Do you believe her?" he asked.

Ellie smiled. "I've never seen anything malevolent, or otherwise, at the manor."

"Nothing?" I clarified.

"I don't know many people that could honestly tell you they haven't at least sensed something wandering the halls here. The land has seen a lot of death. Even railroad workers who perished on the job," she replied, "but at the end of the day, I think it's all just a bunch of nonsense."

***

Cameron and Nolan parked their cars side by side in a municipal lot downtown, and the three of us walked to Lady Perida's shop.

Nolan held the door for Cameron and I as we entered. The smell of sage hung in the dimly lit room and the bells on the door chimed as it fell shut behind us.

"Welcome back," Lady Perida's raspy voice called from behind the moon-phase tapestry. The three of us watched the curtain until it pulled to the side and she emerged.

"We were hoping," Cameron started.

She held up the hand that wasn't supporting her cane and said, "I know why you're here."

"You do?" Nolan questioned.

She sighed, bored. "You don't stay in business long as a fraud."

"Can you tell us what is happening?" I inquired. "Ellie, said you came into contact with something dark there."

She sucked in a breath. Her expression told me I'd brought up an unpleasant memory.

I tried to encourage a response, "Do you know what it is?"

Her face lacked emotion as she spoke, "there is something very dark in the manor. The same darkness that is plaguing Nolan's apartment. If I were you, I'd leave it alone."

"But, what about Martha?" I asked. "Do you know why she's contacting us?"

She scoffed, "you'll never know with *him* in the way."

"Who?" I asked, and she shrugged, unwilling to reveal anything to us.

Cameron stepped toward her. "Can you help us?"

"No," she said, sternly. "If you want answers, you'll have to get them yourselves. But let it be known, I wish you wouldn't."

"If you won't help us, at least tell us what we're up against," I pleaded.

She shook her head. "You're dealing with an incredibly powerful entity. I've tried many times to free Martha from his grasp. It's no use."

"Who is *he*?" I asked, and she shrugged once again.

"What do you mean, free her?" Nolan inquired.

She looked at the front door. "I've said too much already. I told you I cannot be involved. You'll have to find out for yourselves."

The front door to the shop opened, the bells chiming as a group of girls entered. Lady Perida eyed each of us.

"If you'll excuse me, I have appointments to attend to."

***

If it was possible, we exited the shop even more confused than we'd been when we entered. We shared theories as we returned to the parking lot.

"What did she mean by free Martha?" Cameron wondered.

"Maybe she's trapped in the mirror?" I suggested.

Nolan held up a finger and shook it. "No, it can't be that. She's appeared in three different mirrors so far, mine, Zoey's, and the one at the manor."

"True," Cameron agreed.

"So, maybe her reflection is stuck?" I shrugged.

Nolan laughed. "Zo, that sounds ridiculous."

I shrugged. "What do you think it is, then, if you're so smart?"

"Maybe she means she tried to help her get to the afterlife?" Nolan suggested.

Cameron laughed. "Since when are you religious?"

"I'm not...But if you asked me a week ago, I also would have told you I don't believe in ghosts either," he scoffed, "I don't really know what to believe anymore."

We approached the cars, and I got in the passenger side of Nolan's. He opened the driver's side door and looked at Cameron, who had just opened his own door. "Pizza at my place?" he asked.

"Sounds good to me," Cameron nodded before getting into his car.

***

We met Cameron at the door to the apartment and Nolan turned his key just as I finished ordering the pizza.

As the door fell open, the three of us froze, our jaws ajar at the sight of the apartment. Pillow fluff was scattered across the floor, intermingled with shards of broken glass. The coffee table was on its side and the TV was slashed down the middle. In a panic, Nolan ran to his bedroom.

Stepping inside, Cameron and I watched as Nolan frantically searched his bedroom. I moved to the doorway.

"What are you looking for?" I asked.

He lifted a blanket and some clothes from the floor, looking underneath them, then pointed to his nightstand.

"My dad's watch was sitting right here. Grandma gave it to me when he died," he replied.

Cameron came up behind me.

"We should probably call the police, we could be destroying evidence," he suggested.

Just as he finished speaking, a loud crash came from the hallway. Nolan rushed toward it and Cameron and I turned our heads, following his movement.

The dining room table had moved so that it sat upside down against the wall.

I gulped in fear. "You don't think..."

Cameron finished my sentence, "the shadow."

"Where is my watch?" Nolan demanded to the empty hallway.

The lights in the hallway dimmed in response.

Nolan picked up a shoe and threw it down the hallway in anger.

"Show yourself, asshole!" he yelled.

Cameron and I huddled together nervously. He let out a shaky breath.

"Dude, Lady Perida said not to mess with it," Cameron warned him.

Nolan stormed toward the kitchen table and forcefully flipped it upright so that it was no longer blocking the hallway.

"I don't care what Lady Perida said," he barked. "This prick needs to leave us the hell alone."

The building shook, and we held out our arms to steady ourselves against a wall. Cameron looked at Nolan in horror.

"You're pissing it off, dude."

"Bring it on, asshole!" Nolan yelled toward the ceiling.

As if in response to him, a crack appeared on the wall separating the kitchen from the living room. We watched as a kitchen cabinet fell to the floor.

My eyes wide and my breathing heavy, I tried to reason with him, "maybe we should just go to my place."

Ignoring me, he stomped to the bathroom and punched the mirror in anger.

I ran to him and cried, "Nolan, stop! You're going to hurt yourself."

Following me into the bathroom, Cameron leaned down to the bath mat and retrieved something from the floor.

"Is this the watch?" he asked.

Nolan snatched it from his hands and inspected it to ensure it was in one piece. He fumbled with the band as he secured it to his wrist. We stood in silence. I felt the entity leave.

***

A knock came at the door soon after and I said, "that's probably the pizza," as I stepped into the hallway.

I walked to the door and opened it to find a frail man with slicked-back hair and a grumpy expression standing on the sidewalk.

Shoving me aside, he stepped into the living room and looked around, seeming to grow angrier with each step.

Nolan met him in the hallway and he spat, "What the hell have you done to this place?"

Nolan held up his hands defensively and insisted, "it wasn't me."

The man let out an angry grunt. "I suppose it was the resident ghost that trashed my building?"

Cameron let out a snicker, which was met with disgust from the man. "Something funny, carrot top?"

Cameron bit his lip. "No, sir."

The man looked back at Nolan, his boney index finger pointed at Nolan's chest. "I told you one more toe out of line and I'm billing you for it."

"You have to believe me, Mr. Stephens, I didn't do this," he begged, gesturing to the apartment.

"It was like this when we came back," I offered.

"Where are the police, then?" Nolan's landlord quizzed me, turning to view the living room. He held up his hands. "If I came home to my apartment looking like this, I'd call the police."

"I told you we should've called the police," Cameron said, and I nudged him to be quiet.

Nolan sighed, "look, I'll get it cleaned up."

"You're damn right you will," Mr. Stephens snorted, pointing to the cracked wall. "And I expect this to be fixed before you move out."

"Move out!" Nolan exclaimed.

Mr. Stephens grunted. "Your lease is up at the end of the year. It won't be renewed."

With that, he snorted in disgust and exited the apartment, slamming the door shut behind him.

"Fantastic," Nolan said sarcastically, throwing his hands into the air.

Chapter 12

Nolan pulled out his phone and began scrolling through it. I came up behind him and looked over his shoulder at the screen.

"What are you looking at?" I asked.

He continued scrolling as he replied, "I'm trying to see if any earthquakes were reported."

"C'mon dude. You know damn well what happened here. Why won't you just accept that ghosts are real?" Cameron laughed, shaking his head.

Nolan snapped, "Mom wouldn't abandon me!"

"Whoa, calm down," Cameron said, holding up his hands. "No one said anything about your mom."

I placed my arm around Nolan's back. I knew what he meant.

A tear rolled down Nolan's face as he turned into me, wrapping his arms around my back.

He whimpered, "If they're real, why hasn't she contacted me?"

I held him, trying to suppress tears of my own. "Maybe she doesn't know how."

Cameron started to catch on to what was upsetting Nolan. He came closer and put a hand on Nolan's shoulder.

"My parents never contacted me either," he revealed. "I like to tell myself that it's because they've moved on to a better place."

Nolan and I looked up at him sympathetically.

I quietly asked, "What happened to your parents?"

His expression saddened as he replied, "house fire, I was the only one who made it out."

I let a tear fall as I released one arm from Nolan and reached to pull Cameron into a group hug.

As the three of us held each other, Cameron sobbed. "I was only twelve."

Nolan sniffled. "I was ten. My dad murdered her."

They both looked at me to contribute and I said, "my mom died when I was twenty. She hit a deer on her way home from work."

We held each other in solidarity for a few moments before releasing. Cameron wiped his face with his shirt.

"Let's get this mess cleaned up and find us some proof of the paranormal," he said.

Nolan and I nodded and moved to start cleaning the apartment.

***

As I finished replacing the last broken light bulb, Nolan stared up at the crack in his wall.

"What do I do about this?" he asked.

Cameron stood next to us and offered, "my grandpa taught me how to spackle."

I pulled out a chair and sat at the table, opening my phone.

"Let's make a list of things we need to fix the wall, then we can go to the store," I said.

Cameron nodded and started listing items. "Spackle, spackle knife, sponge, drop cloth."

I nodded as I typed his list into my phone. Nolan leaned over to pick up a piece of cardboard from the floor and held it up, revealing the Ouija Board had been snapped in half.

"A new one of these," Nolan said.

Cameron took the broken piece from him and held it up, inspecting it.

"I've got a better idea," he said. "On this ghost show I've been watching, they use this device that scans radio frequencies to communicate with spirits. Let's get one of those instead."

Nolan replied, "if it'll convince Mr. Stephens that I'm not trashing the place I'm in."

***

After a shopping trip, Cameron helped repair Nolan's wall, then he sat at the table to build a DIY version of the ghost communication device.

Cameron rose from the table with a grin and said, "I think it's ready."

Nolan and I, who'd been sitting on the couch, walked over to the table to view Cameron's project.

He pointed to the dial on the cylindrical device. "So this automatically scans through AM frequencies so spirit voices can come through."

Nolan interjected. "Won't we just be hearing radio chatter?"

Cameron glared at him. "No. It scans fast enough that it's not possible to hear human voices. Anything that comes through is a spirit manipulating the frequencies using electromagnetic energy."

Nolan raised an eyebrow. "That doesn't exactly sound very convincing."

"It will when a voice comes through," he retorted. Rolling his eyes at Nolan, he added, "all the big ghost hunters on TV use it. It's called a Phantaphone."

Cameron clicked the device on and white static filled the room. Yelling over the sound, Cameron said, "it's really loud, but the voices are supposed to come through super clear."

I raised an eyebrow and looked at Nolan. Speaking above the static, I said, "I find it hard to believe you can hear anything over that."

Nolan shrugged. "I guess we might as well try?"

"Exactly," Cameron smiled in satisfaction. Then, looking up to the ceiling, he asked, "Shadow ghost, are you here with us?"

We listened intently as the white noise blared from the speaker in Cameron's hand.

He tried again, "What is your name?"

Still, the static remained unchanged.

Nolan gestured toward the room and asked, "Why did you do this?"

A few words garbled out of the machine, and we locked eyes in astonishment.

I looked at Cameron and asked, "Did you catch what it said?"

He shook his head and handed the device to me. "I have an idea. Hold this," he said. Then he pulled the digital recorder out of his pocket and clicked it on. He turned to Nolan and instructed him, "try again. I'll record it so we can play it back."

Nolan took a deep breath before speaking. "Why are you doing this to me?"

After a few moments, the voice came through again. Cameron snatched the Phantaphone from my hands and clicked it off. Then he stopped the digital recorder and rewinded the audio file.

We leaned in, our ears nearly touching. Only the sounds of our breaths could be heard over the static playing from the device.

A voice came through and I snapped my head to look at Cameron.

"I heard, 'away,'" I said.

He rewinded the audio file again, and we held our breath to listen.

The voice came through, "a-way."

"Clear as day," Cameron exclaimed, "it said away."

Nolan's jaw fell open. "Isn't that the same thing the Ouija board said?"

My eyes went wide. He was right. "Yeah."

"Do you think it's the same entity?" Nolan wondered.

Cameron shot Nolan a sly grin. "So it's an entity now?"

Nolan shrugged. "Yeah, yeah, okay. I believe in ghosts. Happy?"

Cameron smiled in satisfaction. "So I was right?"

"I wouldn't go *that* far," I teased.

Looking back at the Phantaphone, Cameron asked, "Martha, is that you?"

"No!" the device clearly spoke, causing us to jolt.

We locked eyes, and Nolan let out a long breath. "So there's more than one spirit?" he asked.

The three of us looked at each other and Cameron broke the silence, "maybe Martha is trying to warn us about the dark entity that Lady Perida told us about."

Nolan stood tall and puffed out his chest, determined to get answers. "If you aren't Martha, then who are you?"

The static dragged on with no spiritual response. After a few more attempts to learn the name of the entity, Cameron turned off both the Phantaphone and the digital recorder.

"What now?" I asked my friends.

"The Meridion manor Halloween party is coming up." Nolan shrugged, pointing to the Phantaphone. "Let's take that with us and see if we can get in contact with Martha."

"Good idea," Cameron said, as we nodded in unison.

***

I wrapped a hair tie around the end of my braid and laughed at Cameron dancing around my living room in excitement.

"I can't believe I get to be Mr. Meridion!" he cheered.

"Who do you think the lucky Mrs. Meridion is?" I joked.

Cameron grinned. "Maybe it'll be that girl that played Martha last year. Wouldn't that be ironic?"

Nolan shook his head. "Maybe this year she'll talk to you without dousing you in wine."

"The ladies love the Cameron special," he rubbed his chest seductively, winking at Nolan.

"Uh huh," Nolan grumbled.

Cameron pretended to kiss the air in between himself and Nolan.

"Do you think Reginald secretly had a thing for Landon Meridion?" Cameron asked me, teasing Nolan, who was dressed as Martha's uncle.

"Oh, definitely," I nodded jokingly, "I mean, look at you. How could anyone resist?"

"Better watch out, Zo, you've got some competition out here." Nolan teased, adjusting the straps on the black suspenders he'd found in a thrift shop.

Cameron eyed Nolan's golden watch. "Hey! That's old and fancy," he said, pointing at it. "Can I wear it tonight? It'll really sell the whole rich businessman look."

"Sure," Nolan laughed, passing the watch to Cameron. "Just don't break it. It was my grandfather's."

"I won't," he assured Nolan.

Joining the two of them in the living room, I clicked the back of my earring into place, completing my outfit. I wore a Victorian dress that I'd crafted myself from thrift store purchases. I'd even sprayed a black temporary dye into my auburn hair to match Martha's. Tonight I was Martha Meridion, and I wanted to get it right.

"You guys ready to go?" I asked.

"Is that..." Cameron started, his eyes wide, "a homemade costume?"

I nodded, spinning around so he could see the floor-length sage gown I'd sewn using my mom's old sewing machine.

"I think it came out nice," I replied with a grin. "It's about time I embrace DIY instead of letting it haunt me."

"I love it!" Cameron said, hugging me.

"It looks great!" Nolan said, gesturing to his thrift-store suit. "It's certainly much better than mine."

I laughed, "with compliments like that, it's no wonder you were Martha's favorite uncle."

***

Much like the last parties we'd attended, Ellie greeted us in the atrium of the manor. Except this time it was more personal.

"Zoey, Nolan, Cameron, it's so nice to see you again," she said.

I smiled and gave her a hug as I said, "it's nice to see you too."

Pulling away to hug each of the boys, she asked, "Have you guys had any luck getting to the bottom of your haunting?"

"Not exactly," Cameron sighed.

Ellie took a moment to explain to a newcomer that they should wait for further instruction, then replied, "that's too bad."

Then she studied my outfit and said, "love the costume, by the way." She nodded in approval as she inspected it further. "Very much something Martha would wear," she added.

I smiled and admitted, "thanks, this is the first time in a long time that I've been excited to dress up."

She pulled at her ruffled skirt. "I adore dressing up. If I could wear this dress every day I would."

We laughed as Nolan pulled at the sleeves of his jacket and joked, "I guess I could get used to this."

As the mumbles of party-goers echoed louder in the room, Ellie backed away from us. "I should get started, people are getting anxious standing around. I'll talk to you guys later."

With that, Ellie turned away from us and clapped three times before giving her speech. As the greeting ended, Cameron turned to Nolan and I.

He spat at Nolan, "I'll have you nowhere near my daughter, brother."

We laughed as he turned to me. "And you, my princess, be a dear and fetch daddy a drink."

Nolan cringed. "Oh dude, don't say that."

"You are definitely not my daddy," I replied, pretending to gag.

"Young lady, don't speak to your father that way." A soft, but familiar voice scolded from behind us.

I turned to see Jaime, the asylum tour guide dressed as Edith Meridion.

I smiled and complimented his costume, "looking good."

He blushed, tucking his chin into the puffy shoulder of his dark blue floral dress.

"Thanks," he said, bashfully. "I've been begging Ellie to let me play Edith for years. Mrs. Meridion is literally my idol."

Nolan chimed in with a rhetorical question, "Who better to play Edith than you?"

"Right?" Jaime nodded, his eyes bright. "Like I spend so much time studying her, I should know everything there is to know about playing her."

"That dress suits you." Cameron winked as he complimented Jaime's attire.

"Thanks," Jaime blushed. "You look quite dapper yourself, Mr. Meridion."

"Why thank you," Cameron gushed, leaning in. "I try hard to impress my beautiful wife."

Jaime giggled.

"Do we need to get you guys a room?" I joked.

Cameron smirked and raised his eyebrows at Jaime. "Maybe," he said.

Distracting from the flirtation, I turned to Jaime to ask about his time at the asylum. "Since we're talking about Mrs. Meridion. I wonder, have you ever tried to make contact with Edith's spirit at the asylum?"

Jaime scoffed and shot me a look, as if to tell me the answer was obvious.

"Of course," he replied. "How do you think I learned so much about her? The best information comes directly from the source."

"Where have you been all my life?" Cameron asked, ogling at Jaime.

Jaime eyed him quizzically.

"Literally no one believes me when I tell them I have talked to ghosts," he explained.

"I believe you," I replied, somewhat offended.

Ignoring me, Cameron grabbed Jaime's wrist and began to lead him away.

"Let's go dear, time for drinks," he said as they disappeared into the kitchen.

I shook my head in amusement as Nolan linked his arm with mine. "How about a drink for the lady?"

I couldn't help but swoon at his words. *Maybe a relationship with him wouldn't be the worst thing in the world*, I thought as I smiled up at him.

"You know, it's officially been a year since we met," I found myself saying.

He used his elbow to pull me closer to his side, then leaned down to whisper, "best year of my life."

I bit my lip in a failed attempt to hide a smile that would resolve any doubt about my feelings for him. I hid my face in his sleeve, and he led me to the kitchen.

***

After helping ourselves to two glasses of wine, we met up with Cameron and Jaime in Martha's room.

As I stepped through the open doorway of the pastel room, Cameron and Jaime hurriedly stood from the bed as if they'd been doing something we weren't supposed to know about.

I raised an eyebrow briefly, and he smiled innocently. I decided not to ask and instead closed the door to the room.

"You brought the Phantaphone, right?" I asked.

Cameron reached into his jacket and procured the device, holding it up for me to see.

"Of course," he replied.

Jaime's eyes lit up. "Oh, a Phantaphone. I've always wanted to use one."

Cameron smiled at Jaime. "I made it myself. We're going to try to contact Martha with it."

Jaime thought for a moment, carelessly swaying side to side as he played with the skirt of his dress.

"I know a few investigators have tried in the past. But I can't remember ever hearing someone say they were successful," Jaime said.

"What do you mean?" I inquired, watching the fabric of his dress move from side to side.

He stopped swaying and approached the mirror. Looking into it, he explained, "As far as I know, no one has ever made contact with Martha."

"I have," I said.

Jaime turned to me, intrigued. "Really?"

I nodded and Cameron gasped, as if he was excited about something. We all turned to face him. He pointed at Jaime.

"You're dressed as Martha's mom. Maybe we can use you as a trigger object," he said.

Nolan raised an eyebrow impatiently. "What are you talking about?"

"Oh, my gosh! Yes!" Jaime emphasized each syllable, ending with his mouth wide open.

I looked at Cameron for an explanation, and he sighed. Then he turned to Jaime and said, "I'm so glad someone gets it. These two are clueless when it comes to the para-normal."

Nolan scoffed, crossing his arms and Cameron continued, "trigger objects are things that remind the ghost of their life. They're supposed to encourage the ghost to make contact with you. Sometimes, they can even use the object's energy to make contact."

"Uh huh," Nolan replied, unconvinced.

Cameron turned the Phantaphone on, filling the room with static noise, and passed the device to Jaime.

Looking into the mirror, the device cradled in his hands, Jaime spoke, "Martha, dear, it's your mother."

We waited, impatiently peering over Jaime's shoulder to see if Martha would appear.

Jaime tried again, "Martha, come say hello, please."

A spark of curiosity fell over Nolan and he gently pushed Jaime to the side, staring into the mirror.

"Martha, it's me, uncle Reginald," he said.

As if on cue, Martha's face materialized in the mirror.

Her soft expression turned to a sneer as her eyes met Nolan's. She began to fade, and I stepped next to Nolan.

"Please don't go, we just want to know what is going on," I said.

Cameron squeezed in between us and Jaime balanced on his toes to get a better look at the mirror.

Cameron almost yelled into the mirror, "It's Martha!"

She angrily placed a finger over her lips to silence him and he lowered his voice to a whisper, cowering as he did. "Sorry, I just..."

His words were cut off by the blaring of the manor's fire alarm system. We all jumped as Martha disappeared and Jaime ushered us toward the bedroom door.

Nolan hesitated at the door. "You're not supposed to open doors when there's a fire, right?" he asked.

Cameron shoved past him, throwing the door open, and rushed down the hall, practically falling face first down the steps. We followed him out the front door of the manor and stood, our backs to each other, scanning the property for any sign of Cameron. Nolan breathed heavily as he looked for his friend.

"We need to find him," Nolan stated, "I think he's having another episode."

"Episode?" Jaime looked concerned as he placed his right hand over his heart and peered toward the orchard.

Nolan nodded. "He survived a house fire when he was little. He's got PTSD from it. We have to find him before he gets hurt, or worse."

I approached a group of girls in the parking lot and described Cameron to them.

"Have you seen him?" I asked.

They shook their heads and resumed muttering about the inconvenience of the fire alarm.

"There's clearly no fire. Ugh, so annoying," one girl said.

I rolled my eyes as I returned to Nolan and Jaime.

"He didn't go toward the parking lot," said.

I looked toward the orchard and pointed into the shadows. "He must've gone that way."

Chapter 13

Nolan led the way, charging toward the vast array of apple trees.

"Cam!" he called out as he marched, Jaime and I at his heels.

We reached the tree line, and a chill overcame us. Each of us shivered.

Nolan tried one last time for a reply, "Cameron, can you hear me?"

When no response came, Nolan muttered, "fuck," under his breath.

I grabbed his arm. As much as I hated to admit it, I was a little intimidated by the dark orchard. Jaime must have been too, because when an owl let out a soft hoot above our heads, Jaime lunged toward me, wrapping his arms around my waist in fear.

A branch cracked in front of us and Jaime's cheek touched mine as he clung tighter to me.

With a shaking voice, he whispered, "What was that?"

"I stepped on a stick," Nolan hissed, "shut up. We need to be able to hear Cameron."

We stood at the edge of the orchard, huddled together in silence, hoping to hear Cameron's voice. Finally, Nolan shook his arm free and turned to us.

"Stay here. I'm going to look for him," he said.

I grabbed his arm and replied, "no, I'm coming with you."

Jaime let his arms fall against the fabric of his skirt and looked back at the manor. He studied the distance between us and the building, then gulped, "I don't want to walk back there alone, I'm coming too."

I took a deep breath and reached for Jaime's hand, our fingers interlacing.

"We have to stick together, or we could all end up lost," I said.

"Yeah, the estate has over 250 acres of land," Jaime informed us.

Nolan sighed, "great that means he could be anywhere."

***

Nolan reached for my free hand and the three of us stood in a line facing the trees. Taking a deep breath, we set off through the orchard, under the canopy of thousands of honey crisp trees.

Nolan led the way, ducking under branches, his hand still entwined with mine as he walked slightly ahead of Jaime and I. Jaime clung tight to me as we trekked.

A thump sounded to our right, and we all froze. A leaf rustled from the same area and Jaime huddled closer to me, wrapping his hands around my bicep.

Nolan whispered, "it was just an apple falling, let's go."

Jaime let out a shaky breath and reluctantly stepped with me, his chest against my arm.

We trekked deeper into the orchard until the manor was no longer visible behind us. The moonlight peeking through the leaves was the only thing lighting our path.

Another apple fell ahead of us and Jaime stopped in his tracks.

"Can't we use a flashlight or something? I feel like I'm in a horror movie," he whispered.

Sirens sounded in the distance, likely the fire department coming to address the false alarm, and I agreed with Jaime, "it is really creepy out here."

Nolan pulled his phone from his pocket and turned the flashlight on, illuminating the path ahead.

A branch cracked in the distance and Nolan called out, "Cameron?"

"What was that?" Jaime exclaimed, taking a step back in fear. He dragged me with him as sirens blared closer.

A voice replied from the distance, barely audible over the fire trucks.

"What did he say?" Nolan asked the two of us.

I shook my head, uncertain. "Something about tracks, I think."

"The railroad tracks!" Jaime exclaimed in a whisper.

"Cameron?" Nolan called out again.

"Over here," a faint voice responded in the distance. We took off running toward the sound, my hand linked with Jaime's

As we moved closer to the area the voice had come from, the sirens ceased and the orchard went silent.

Jaime gulped as we followed Nolan deeper into the sea of trees. We came to the edge of a clearing and paused under the cover of darkness that the trees provided.

Nolan stood with Jaime and I huddled at his heels. He shook his arm free of my grip and bravely stepped into the clearing, looking left and then right. Jaime and I hesitantly followed suit.

In the center of the clearing, running parallel to the tree line, were railroad tracks as far as the moonlight shined.

A distorted shadow figure moved to our left, about one hundred yards from where we were standing. Jaime and I clung to each other, and I whispered in his ear as quietly as I could, "What is that?"

"Oh my god," Jaime whimpered, trying to stay quiet, "is that a skin walker?"

"It looks like a person," I cautiously whispered back, Jaime's nails digging into my skin.

"Cameron?" Nolan called out, causing us to jump.

Jaime shrieked as the figure's head turned toward us.

"Nolan?" Cameron replied.

We sighed in relief as the name echoed toward us. Jaime and I let go of each other and ran to meet Cameron, who was sitting on the railroad tracks.

Nolan's flashlight lit up Cameron's face, and he winced at the light as we got closer. Nolan flipped off the light and squatted in front of Cameron.

He placed a hand on Cameron's shoulder and asked, "Are you okay?"

It was evident that he'd been crying, watermarks lined his cheeks. He nodded.

Nolan joined him on the rail, and Jaime and I stepped closer. Facing the two of them, we knelt down, unsure of what to say.

Nolan asked, "What happened, man?"

Cameron burst into tears and he replied, "I don't know, I just...just the...the fire alarm went off and I... I don't know..."

Nolan hugged him from the side, and I bit my lip to hold back a sympathetic tear.

"It's okay Cam. We're here for you," Nolan assured him.

Jaime and I nodded in support and Nolan turned to Jaime to fill him in. "Cameron's house burned down when he was little."

Jaime placed one hand over his mouth in sympathy and reached for Cameron's hand with the other. "I'm so sorry," he whispered.

Cameron sniffled. "my parents died in the fire."

Jaime nodded.

Understanding that Cameron was struggling for words, Nolan continued, "he gets triggered sometimes. It's still hard for him, even all these years later."

Cameron nodded, letting out a shaky breath. Jaime placed a hand on Cameron's cheek.

"You don't have to explain anything to me. I'm just glad you're okay."

I studied the grass peeking up through the tracks and scanned the tree line. "Why did you run into the orchard, of all places?"

Cameron furrowed his brows as if he was trying to remember. "I don't know. I guess I kind of blacked out."

Nolan raised an eyebrow. "What do you mean, you blacked out?"

He shrugged. "I don't remember running into the woods. I just remember following him to the railroad tracks and then I heard you calling my name."

Jaime's eyes went wide, and he looked around frantically. "Who did you follow?"

"Him." Cameron pointed to his wrist just as an assortment of apples fell to the ground behind us. Jaime and I turned in a panic, terrified that we could be coming face to face with a skinwalker.

Nolan sighed, "apples guys, we're in an orchard."

"Where is the person you followed now?" I asked, and he held up Nolan's watch.

A faint white figure in a tattered button-down shirt stared back at us from the face of Nolan's watch.

Jaime and I scooted forward until we were huddled against Nolan and Cameron.

Wide-eyed, Jaime let out a delayed scream, and the figure spoke calmly, "you must leave the orchard, it is not safe for you."

It began to dissipate and Nolan yelled. "Wait! Who are you?"

The figure hung, just barely visible. "My name is Reginald. I must go."

Nolan looked at Cameron's wrist and then at us. "Did we just see the ghost of Reginald Bauer?"

Jaime lifted Cameron's wrist and inspected the watch.

Tapping the glass face, his mouth hung open. "Where did you get this?" he asked.

Nolan shrugged. "It was my grandpa's. I got it when he died. Why?"

Jaime tapped the watch face twice more, and he shakily explained, "this watch belonged to Reginald Bauer." He held up Cameron's wrist, twisting it so that we could see the watch face, and tapped it once more. "See the inscription on the face, RB."

"I thought RB was for my grandpa, Robert Bauer," Nolan replied skeptically.

Jaime shook his head. "No. This watch definitely belonged to Reginald Bauer, no doubt."

I raised an eyebrow. "What makes you so sure?"

Jaime explained. "It was a one of a kind piece, crafted by the famed watch maker Forrester O'Donnell in the 1800s. Arthur Meridion, Landon's father, gifted it to Reginald on his 21st birthday. It's been missing for centuries," he added.

Nolan looked at the watch, nodding as he started to put the pieces together. "But if Reginald was murdered, he was probably wearing this watch when he died, so how did I end up with it?"

Jaime inspected the watch. "It's so shiny."

Cameron replied, "I cleaned it before we came."

"What kind of cleaner did you use? I've been wanting to clean mine," Jaime replied, holding up the watch on his right wrist.

I interrupted them, "Can we get back on topic?

Jaime, what makes you so sure it's Reginald's watch?"

Jaime bit his lip and dropped his wrist to his side, hiding it in the skirt of his dress. He took a breath before replying, "it's said to be infused with lilac."

"What does lilac have to do with anything?" I asked.

Jaime smiled, excitedly. "Lilac is said to promote spiritual communication."

"So you think the watch is a supercharged trigger object?" I confirmed.

Jaime nodded with a smile.

"Why would he lead me here?" Cameron asked.

"What exactly do you mean, when you say he led you here?" I asked.

"He told me which way to walk," Cameron explained.

Nolan eyed him skeptically. "A spirit led you into the woods? It sounds like you've been reading too much Stephen King."

Cameron rolled his eyes. "I swear Reginald led me here."

"Why would he lead you to the railroad tracks?" I repeated his question

.

Cameron shrugged. "I don't know. But it's not the first time it's happened to me. Toby led me out of the fire when I was five."

"The clown?" I clarified.

He nodded. "Yeah, I wouldn't have made it out of the house if it weren't for him."

He gazed up at the moon in thought. "I wonder if he's still there?"

I looked around the clearing. To our right, a rectangular object protruded from the Earth. I pointed to it as I spoke, "Guys, what is that?"

The three of them turned toward the area I was pointing to. Squinting into the moonlit clearing, Nolan replied, "I have no idea."

"It looks like a rock," Jaime said.

Cameron stood and began walking toward the object. "One way to find out," he said.

The three of us stood to follow Cameron toward the stone-like object. As we approached, we discovered two small stacks of smooth, round stones. A bouquet of wilting wildflowers lay between the stacks, a note tied to the stems.

I knelt down to pick up the letter and carefully unrolled it.

"What does it say?" Cameron peered over my shoulder, Jaime hanging off his arm for comfort.

I began to read it aloud, "Dearest Grandfather, Nolan Bauer has discovered his ties to the manor and seems determined to contact you. I fear Uncle Landon has caught on. I beg you to protect them from his wrath. Love, Luisa."

Nolan took the note from me and read it over. Looking up from the paper, he asked, "Who is Luisa?"

"And why is she leaving notes to her grandfather out here?" I added.

"Maybe her grandfather was one of the railroad workers that died," Cameron suggested.

We all looked at Jaime for an explanation. He shrugged. "I've never heard of someone named Luisa Meridion, or Luisa Bauer, for that matter."

Nolan pointed to the stones. "These are used in ancient rituals, they're called cairns. Sometimes people use them to mark burial sites or trails. Maybe we can find more and follow them to the answer?"

I knelt down in front of the stone towers and a feeling of imminent danger came over me.

"Something doesn't feel right. I think we should just go back to the manor," I said cautiously.

"I agree," Jaime enthusiastically replied.

"Maybe we can ask Ellie," I suggested.

We agreed to reconvene with Ellie back at the manor, then set off back into the orchard.

***

Cameron huffed as the manor came into view and we emerged from the trees. "What time is it?" he asked.

Nolan looked down at the watch Cameron had returned to him.

"Three in the morning," he replied.

"I didn't realize we were out there that long," I commented and Jaime nodded in agreement.

Cameron looked at the ground. "Yeah, sorry. I guess it's kind of my fault."

"Don't worry about it," Nolan placed a hand on his shoulder. "We're just glad you're okay."

We walked toward the parking lot and stopped at Nolan's car. "I guess we'll have to talk to Ellie tomorrow," he said, unlocking the doors.

I looked at Cameron. "Meet back here at 11am?"

"Sure," he nodded. Then he looked at Jaime. "Do you want to come too?"

He shrugged, "sure."

"Cool," Cameron smiled, looking back at Nolan. "Can I get a ride home?"

Jaime spoke before Nolan could respond, "I'll give you a ride."

Cameron hesitated and Jaime assured him, "I really don't mind."

"Thanks," Cameron replied, walking with Jaime to his car.

Chapter 14

The next morning, Nolan and I met Jaime and Cameron in the parking lot of the manor.

Jaime held up his hands as he emerged from his car, and said, "we're not talking about my face. I ran out of makeup remover, end of discussion."

"Alright, then," Nolan laughed.

I bit my lip to stifle a laugh as I looked at the black smudge under each of his eyes. I reached into my backpack and pulled out a small container of makeup remover wipes.

"Here, you can borrow these," I said.

He let out a breath of relief. "You're a lifesaver," he said. Then, he opened his car door and sat in the driver's seat, pulling the visor down.

"You have no idea how happy this makes me," he said as he used the small mirror to clean the mascara underneath his eyes.

When he was done, he handed the wipes back to me and grabbed an eye pencil from his center console. Nolan watched impatiently as he redid his eye makeup and brushed his hair out of his face as he checked each angle.

"Perfect," he announced, slamming his car door as he stood.

"Ready?" Nolan asked impatiently.

"Ready," Jaime confirmed.

Cameron led the way as we approached the manor and held the door for the three of us. We entered and quickly located Ellie in the sitting room.

"Hi guys," she said, looking up from her book, surprised to see us. "What brings you back so soon?"

The four of us looked at each other, realizing that we probably should have talked about what we were going to say before entering.

"Umm," I hesitated.

Nolan chimed in, "one of my students wanted to know a little bit about the manor. I promised I'd ask you her questions, but I woke up this morning and realized I forgot to."

She straightened her posture in delight and gestured to the surrounding chairs. "Please, sit. I'd be happy to tell you anything I can."

Jaime and I shrugged at each other and moved toward the chairs, going along with Nolan's plan.

Ellie grinned, lifting her tea mug. "Tea, anyone?"

"No, thanks," we each mumbled.

"More for me," she shrugged. "What was it your students wanted to know?"

Nolan paused, planning out the interview in his head. "Have you ever heard of someone named Luisa?"

Ellie brought her chin to her chest and her eyes widened, she seemed surprised. "I haven't heard that name in a long time."

Cameron leaned forward, resting his elbows on his knees.

She continued, "Luisa Orlander, I assume, is who you're referring to."

I looked at Nolan. The name still wasn't familiar. She clarified, "Luisa was Reginald Bauer's granddaughter."

"She's related to you," Cameron looked at Nolan, excited.

"Your last name is Bauer?" Jaime's jaw dropped.

"Who is your father?" Ellie asked. "There's a family tree upstairs. Maybe we can trace it back."

Nolan looked at the floor, his father had always been a sore subject. I rubbed his back as he decided how much to share.

He sighed as he said his father's name. "Tom Bauer."

Jaime and Ellie both sucked their lips in. They clearly recognized the name. But, how could they not? The murder was all over the news when it happened.

Nolan offered, "I promise, I'm nothing like him."

Ellie looked horrified, "oh, no I didn't think..."

"It's fine, I'm used to it," Nolan waved it off. "You said there's a family tree?"

She nodded and stood from the couch. "Yes. Come with me."

We followed her to Edith's study and watched as she scanned the shelves.

"Here it is," she said, removing an old black leather-bound book from the shelf.

I eyed Nolan and leaned close to whisper in his ear, "that's the book from Valentine's Day."

He nodded as Ellie read the title out loud, "Families Of The Lackawanna Railroad."

Ellie flipped to a section discussing Arthur Meridion and stopped on a page that featured a family tree.

She moved to the small card table and set the book down so we could all see.

Pointing to the most recent entry with her index finger, she said, "The last descendant listed here is Lucius Bauer, who died in 1961."

She looked at Nolan, and he shook his head. "Never heard of him."

Jaime pulled out his phone and began furiously typing. After a few seconds, he pointed to the screen. "I found the rest on this ancestry site." He set his phone next to the book, and we followed along.

"Okay, so Johnson Orlander married Perida Bauer, and they had Luisa Bauer, who married Carl Smith," I explained as I compared the two family trees.

Nolan pointed to the last entry. "Robert Bauer, born in 1940. That's my grandfather!"

We looked at Luisa's name under Reginald and followed the line back to her parents. "Perida and Johnson Orlander," I added, "and Reginald is her father."

"I wonder if she's related to Lady Perida," Cameron chimed in.

"Perida was a very common name around here," Ellie informed him.

"So wait." Nolan pushed in front of us to inspect the family trees. "So Reginald Bauer is actually related to me."

Jaime nodded. "That's crazy."

Nolan thought for a moment and appeared to be calculating in his mind. "Reginald is my great-great-great-grandfather, and whoever Luisa is…" he trailed off.

"She's your great-great-aunt!" I exclaimed.

Ellie nodded, clearly impressed. "If you two want a job at the manor, we could always use someone so quick with lineage."

He shrugged. "I took a class on it in college."

"Wait," Jaime said, holding up a finger. "Something isn't making sense."

We looked at him, waiting for him to explain. He finally did, "If Reginald's direct descendants are all daughters who married, then why is the Bauer name still being used?"

We looked at Ellie, hoping she'd have an answer. She read through the family tree and said, "interesting."

Then she looked up from the book and replied, "my best guess would be that it became somewhat of a family tradition after Reginald assumed Loretta's name."

"My mom took my dad's name," Nolan said.

"But you didn't know your grandparents, right?" I asked.

"So maybe the tradition stopped," I suggested.

Cameron looked at Ellie and then Nolan and, unable to hold it in any longer, exclaimed, "Why are we not talking about the fact that Nolan is literally related to Reginald Bauer?"

"Calm down Cam, this doesn't mean anything," Nolan insisted.

"What do you mean?" Cameron replied, "this could explain why you're being haunted."

"Let's not get ahead of ourselves," Nolan replied.

"Luisa died in 1991," I said, pointing at her entry. "Maybe she still has relatives in town."

Ellie searched something on her phone and said, "there's an address for her in the town records. You could stop by and see if the current owner knows anything."

The four of us looked at each other and nodded in agreement. I looked at Ellie and said, "thank you for all of your help."

She shrugged, "anytime."

***

We piled into Nolan's car, leaving Jaime's behind at the manor, and Nolan put the address Ellie had given us into his navigation app.

The four of us rode in silence, processing the new revelations. I wondered what we would say if someone actually opened the door for us at Luisa's former residence.

Nolan parked on the street outside the old home. The three-story building was grey with pink trim, the paint inches thick from the many times it had been done over.

Cameron stepped up to the concrete landing in front of the door and turned to us, looking nervous. He broke the tension with a joke.

"Should I offer them the Cameron special?"

Jaime looked confused. I rolled my eyes and said, "trust me, you don't want to know."

Cameron winked at Jaime. "Or maybe he does."

"Just knock," Nolan groaned.

Cameron let out a quick breath and knocked twice. The three of us stepped forward, so we were all in a line as we waited for the door to open.

***

We heard wooden planks creaking as it seemed someone was descending the home's centuries-old staircase. The tap of a cane hitting the planks of the first floor sounded, followed by two heavy footsteps.

The click of the cane got closer, and we each took a step back as the deadbolt released. The door pulled open slowly, revealing a familiar amethyst cane, partially masked by a lavender sleeve. I looked up at the person's face. Her gray hair, streaked with remnants of tan poking out from the loose hair clip at the back of her head.

"Lady Perida," Cameron said softly, with a hint of surprise.

Her eyes drooped, and she slouched her back as her gaze fell upon us. She clearly wasn't amused to be seeing us.

"I told you, I can't help you," she muttered impatiently, stepping backward, her hand on the doorknob.

"Please," I begged her not to close the door. "We just have a few questions, and then we'll leave you alone."

Cameron gave her a pleading look, and she sighed with her whole body.

"Fine," she stepped aside, "come in."

Without giving her time to change her mind, we stepped inside the floorboards creaking with each footfall.

She led us to the kitchen and waved to the table. "Sit."

We obeyed, and she poured a mug of tea for each of us, setting the cups on the table. The four of us waited to see if she would speak first. We were all curious to see if she knew why we had come.

She sat between Nolan and Jaime. Across from them, Cameron and I sat eagerly awaiting her next words.

She let out a breath. "I suppose you're looking for Luisa Orlander." It was more of a statement than a question.

We nodded.

"Well, you've found her," she said, a hint of annoyance in her tone.

The four of us perked up, our eyes sparkling with interest. I broke the silence that followed, "You're Luisa Orlander?"

She nodded, and Cameron looked perplexed.

"But how is that possible? She died over twenty years ago," he asked.

A look of amusement showed on her face, with a smile threatening to form.

"Luisa Perida Orlander the second," she said, her hand on the center of her chest. "My mother, Luisa Perida Orlander, died in 1991. My grandmother, Perida Bauer-Orlander in 1982."

Nolan brought his hands to his face and moved them as if he was wiping off sweat from a long, hard workday. His hands covering his mouth, he looked up at Lady Perida. "Is there anyone in this town I'm not related to?"

Cameron snickered. "Wouldn't it be funny if you were related to Zoey?"

I shot him a glare. "Not funny."

He grinned, raising his eyebrows and quietly muttered, "it'd be a little funny."

Rolling my eyes, I turned to Lady Perida. I had so many questions I wasn't sure where to start.

She didn't wait for me, she explained, "my great-grandfather was Reginald Bauer, formerly Meridion. After being outcast from the Meridion family, he took on his wife's maiden name, Bauer."

She turned her head to look at Nolan, adding, "and yes, to confirm your suspicions, I am your great aunt. I'm glad to finally have a chance to get to know you."

He snorted in response and looked away.

"How long have you known this?" I wondered aloud.

Cameron added a question of his own. "Why didn't you tell us at the shop?"

"Why didn't you contact me when your niece died?" Nolan spat, "Or how about when your sister died?"

"Nolan," I tried to calm him, placing a hand on his shoulder.

He flinched away from my touch.

He threw words at Lady Perida, "don't act like I'm some long-lost relative you didn't know about. You know when I walk into a room, now you're going to tell me you magically somehow didn't figure out I was your nephew?"

I grabbed his arm in an attempt to quiet him, and to my amazement, it worked. He stopped talking and relaxed into the chair, refusing to look at the psychic.

"Just let her explain," I pleaded with him, "I'm sure she has a good reason for all of it."

"Of course I knew," she replied. "Your father didn't want me around you, said he didn't want a devil worshipper speaking with his son or some nonsense."

"He's been in jail for years," Nolan retorted. "Where were you then?"

"I didn't want to disrupt your life," she calmly explained.

He scoffed and crossed his arms, looking at the wall, much like a toddler would during a temper tantrum.

"Sorry to interrupt," Jaime said, "but question...what's with the Bauer name being passed down by women?"

Lady Perida laughed as if his trivial question was the last thing on her mind. She replied, "Reginald instilled a sense of pride in the name that was passed down through generations."

She shrugged. "I guess none of us wanted to give it up."

"They can have it," Nolan muttered.

Cameron raised his eyebrows as if to say, 'alrighty then' and turned to the psychic.

"Anyway. Why didn't you tell us about all of this when we were at the shop?" he asked.

She pursed her lips like a disappointed parent and replied, "I was hoping you would be smart enough to heed my warning and stay out of it."

"Stay out of what?" I asked?

She let out a breath of defeat. "Well, I suppose there's no point in hiding it from you now. You'll find out yourselves soon enough."

"Find out what?" I asked impatiently.

She eyed me, unamused. "The Meridion family has many secrets. Secrets they've kept hidden for over a century. I will tell you what I've learned, but you must understand, I cannot support you in meddling with these spirits. We're not talking about friendly ghosts, there is a very powerful entity within that manor. You must refrain from agitating it any further."

Nolan pleaded, "look, I'm not trying to stir up any ancient spirits. I just want to know what the hell is going on."

"Very well," she conceded. "Arthur Meridion purchased the land on which the Meridion manor sits just as plans were being drawn for the Lackawanna railroad. Of course, he was well aware his land sat directly in the line where the tracks were to be laid and made a deal with the railroad to allow them to build their tracks straight through the center of his recently planted orchard."

Jaime nodded along with her story, he was very familiar with the history she'd shared thus far.

Nolan tried to rush her, "yeah, yeah, we know about the railroad. What does that have to do with the ghost in my apartment?"

Lady Perida glared at him. "I'm getting there," she replied.

With a huff, she continued, "Arthur Meridion had two sons, Landon, the oldest, and Reginald. By the time Reginald came of age to marry, neither he nor Landon had found a wife. Arthur decided to help them out by hosting a ball at the manor, inviting prestigious families from all over the region."

She looked at each of us as if to make sure we were paying attention. "Now, at the ball, was Edith Sullivan, the daughter of a wealthy oil mogul from New England," she explained. "Edith caught the eye of both of the Meridion brothers that night."

Cameron cut her off, "but she ended up with Landon, right?"

Lady Perida eyed him impatiently. "Edith fell in love with Reginald, they snuck off into the orchard that night and just a few weeks later a fight broke out between the two brothers. Arthur stepped in and demanded that Reginald heed to his brother and allow him to take Edith's hand in marriage. Landon, of course, was thrilled, he'd have a wife, potential heirs to the Meridion name, and most importantly a claim to the manor. Reginald, on the other hand, was furious. He went straight to his father and revealed that Edith was already carrying his child."

We all gasped. Jaime threw his hands up, nearly smacking Cameron in the face.

"What happened to the baby?" I urged her to continue.

"Arthur was disgusted with his son's behavior. He arranged for Edith to marry Landon promptly and claim the child was his. Reginald was written out of the will," she explained.

"Then what?" I asked, on the edge of my seat.

She smiled at my enthusiasm and continued, "about a year later, out of spite, Reginald married Loretta Bauer, the daughter of one of Arthur's enemies. He assumed Loretta's name in an attempt to distance himself from the Meridion family and the two welcomed a daughter not long after."

She ended with, "her name was Perida Bauer."

Nolan nodded, adding up the information in his head.

"So you're Reginald's great-granddaughter?" Cameron interjected, and she nodded.

"Did you write the note?" I asked, assuming she'd know what note I was referring to.

She sighed. "You've been to his grave?"

Jaime looked confused. "We didn't go to the cemetery. We found it in the orchard."

"Wait!" I gasped. "He's actually buried under the railroad?"

She laughed, as if amused by our ignorance. "I placed the note with two cairns. My grandfather was buried in an unmarked grave under a honey crisp tree, not far from the tracks."

I interrupted her, "but I thought the body was never found."

"Oh, it was," she confirmed.

"When?" Jaime asked, taken aback by the news.

"I read the newspaper every morning," Nolan replied skeptically, "I've never seen anything about a body being found at the manor."

"Martha found him," Lady Perida replied.

I nodded in understanding as the truth came over me.

"She found it when she went looking for her mother?" I confirmed.

Lady Perida nodded.

"Wait, hold up, I think I just realized something." Jaime held up his hands, his elbows resting on the table. "Was Reginald Martha's real father?"

Lady Perida smiled as the pieces of the puzzle started to come together. Then her expression became stern.

"I can't answer that," she said.

I gasped in a breath of air. "That must be why Martha is trying to contact us. So we could know the truth."

Nolan nodded, his eyes glued to the ceiling in thought. He didn't say a word.

Cameron furrowed his brow, contemplating something. "So...but...that still doesn't explain the shadow figure."

Lady Perida shot him an insightful smirk and turned to Nolan, staring him down until he met her eyes.

"So you've seen him too?" she asked.

"Who?" I asked, desperate for an answer as Nolan did his best to ignore her.

She lifted her shoulders as she sucked in a breath and let them relax as she exhaled. Then she looked around the table at us.

"There is something very dark haunting this town," she explained, periodically locking eyes with each of us as she continued to relay her theory. We leaned into her words. "That something is Landon Meridion."

We gasped, and Jaime smacked his palm against the tabletop.

Lady Perida paused, allowing us to calm ourselves. "I have been to the manor and sensed the spirits there. Three to be exact. One I believe to be Martha."

I jumped in, "we saw her!"

She nodded, "another, is Reginald."

Cameron, excited, added, "we saw him too!"

"And Landon is the third?" I assumed.

"Yes," she said simply.

I turned to Nolan and waited for his eyes to fall on me.

"That must be who we saw," I said.

Jaime let out a thoughtful hum, and we turned to him as he inquired about his favorite Meridion. "Edith must be attached to the asylum? That's why she doesn't appear at the manor?"

"Spirits tend to stay in the location that meant the most to them," Lady Perida explained.

"Edith hated the manor," Jaime confirmed. "She told me she preferred the asylum."

"You've spoken to Edith Meridion?" Lady Perida asked, seemingly surprised.

Jaime nodded. "She talks to me through the mirror," he replied.

Lady Perida nodded and sat up straighter. "My grandmother believed that spirits could communicate through mirrors, a kind of ancient video call, if you will."

"Martha appeared in my mirror," I blurted. "That's how we got involved in this whole thing in the first place."

"Interesting," Lady Perida nodded in thought.

"But I still don't understand why she came to me. Shouldn't she have gone to Nolan first?" I inquired.

Lady Perida looked at Nolan. "I suspect it has something to do with Nolan's skepticism. Maybe Martha thought it would be easier to get through to him by connecting with you."

Cameron thought. "But Zoey and Nolan weren't even dating yet."

Jaime held his palms to the sky as he spoke. "Why don't we just go ask Martha?"

"We tried," Cameron said with a sigh, "she won't talk to us."

"So, let's try again," Jaime suggested.

We looked at Lady Perida. "Can't you help us get in contact with her?"

She shook her head. "As I said before, if you want to pursue this, you must do it without my help."

With that, she stood and announced, "I think it's time I get down to the shop. I wish you luck."

We understood it was time for us to leave and stood to move toward the front door. We paused on the front landing and I turned to Lady Perida.

"Thank you for sharing what you know about the manor," I said.

She nodded and closed the door as we turned to walk back to the car.

Chapter 15

The four of us sat in Nolan's living room, trying to decide how to proceed.

"Maybe we should just stay out of it, like Lady Perida said," Nolan suggested, accepting the fact that we may be in over our heads.

"We can't just give up," Cameron insisted, "maybe Martha really needs our help."

Jaime nodded, "yeah, I wouldn't want to find out we left her, or Edith, in trouble."

"So what," Nolan said, "We're just going to risk our lives for a couple dead people?"

The three of us each shot him a grimace, and I replied, "Wouldn't you want someone to help you, if you were in their situation?"

Nolan opened his mouth to respond, but no words came out. He shut his lips and Jaime asked, "So what are we going to do?"

Cameron stood and announced, "if Lady Perida isn't going to help us, we'll just have to do it ourselves."

"And how do you propose we do that?" Nolan asked, a hardness to his tone.

Cameron glared at him, and then a sly grin formed on his face.

"I say we go find Ellie. It's about time some real ghost hunting went down at Meridion Manor," he said.

Jaime lifted his shoulders in excitement. "Oh, I do love a good ghost hunt," he said, "I used to lead flashlight tours at the asylum when I worked nights."

Cameron lifted his infrared camera. "I've been wanting to put this thing to use," he replied.

Nolan looked at me skeptically, and I shrugged. "It could be fun."

He threw up his hands in defeat. "Alright, I guess let's go talk to Ellie."

Cameron's grin expanded across his face as he turned toward the front door.

"I'll go get the Phantaphone," he said, turning to leave.

He paused with his hand on the doorknob and said, "hmm, we might have a problem."

"What?" Jaime asked.

Cameron smiled innocently. "I think I might've left the Phantaphone in Martha's room," he admitted.

Nolan sighed. "Well, at least we can get it while we're there."

***

We rushed to the front door of the manor, and Cameron practically threw it open in excitement. He'd been begging us to ghost hunt with him for months, and now that it was finally happening, he was nearly impossible to contain.

Ellie stepped out of her office upon hearing the door creak shut behind us and cheerily greeted us, "Hey, guys!"

I smiled back at her and allowed Cameron to take the lead.

"Can we do a ghost hunt at the manor?" he excitedly asked, his hands clasped together as if he was begging.

Ellie's face was full of regret. She bit her lower lip like she didn't know how to say what she needed to. After a long pause, she finally replied, "I'm sorry guys, the historical society doesn't allow ghost hunts."

"But..." Cameron started, his shoulders slumping as he realized it was no use arguing. "Why not?"

"I don't know the full story," she replied, taking a breath before continuing. "There was an incident with Lady Perida years ago and they've banned ghost hunters and psychics ever since."

"That's odd," I replied.

Ellie shrugged. "I wish I could help, but there's honestly nothing I can do about it."

Cameron sighed, so Ellie added, "you could try asking Lady Perida what happened, if you really want to know."

A snort of laughter escaped Nolan, and I shot him a look of disapproval.

We all knew there was nothing Ellie could do to change the rules and we'd never ask her to put her job in jeopardy for us.

"Thanks for trying to help," Jaime offered.

She forced a sympathetic smile and replied, "of course."

The four of us retreated to the parking lot, our heads hung in disappointment. As we approached Nolan's car, Cameron muttered, "I'm never going to get to do a proper ghost hunt."

Jaime placed a hand on Cameron's shoulder. "You will, someday," he said.

Cameron smiled at him, and the four of us got back into the car.

***

We arrived back at Nolan's apartment and brainstormed how to proceed as we waited for our food order to arrive.

"Maybe we can go to the board of directors for the historical society," Cameron suggested.

I thought for a moment. "I feel like that's a bit extreme," I replied.

Jaime searched the ceiling for ideas and then held up his index finger.

"What if we go to the next manor party and lock ourselves in Martha's room? They'd never know what we're doing in there," Jaime said.

Cameron replied, "I like that idea."

Nolan chimed in, sarcastically, "because that worked so well last time."

Cameron threw his hands down on the dining table angrily, and we all jumped.

"I forgot to get the Phantaphone while we were there," he explained.

"Okay, this is totally crazy," I said, dismissing his outburst. "But what if we sneak into the manor tonight and do a ghost hunt?"

"Without permission?" Cameron clarified.

I nodded.

"Who are you and what have you done with Zoey?" he joked.

I shrugged. "We want answers. It's the only way we're going to get them."

Jaime and Cameron looked at each other and shrugged, then the three of us turned to Nolan, who was fidgeting with his keys.

He let out a breath and replied, "unless anyone has a better idea, I guess we don't have much of a choice."

Cameron's face lit up with a smile, and he stood from the table.

"I'll get the camera ready," he said.

Our food arrived as Cameron prepped his gear. He plugged each battery in to ensure they were fully charged for the night ahead. We ate and watched a movie until it was dark outside, then ordered a ride to a small abandoned farmhouse on the opposite side of the orchard from where the manor sat. We decided it was the best way to ensure that our cars wouldn't be spotted, giving us away.

Throughout the car ride, the four of us relayed an elaborate story to the driver about how we were hunting for Appalachian monsters in the woods. He seemed to find our story plausible and wished us luck through the open passenger window before driving off. We watched the car speed down the road until the taillights were no longer visible, then set off into the orchard.

Through the quiet, a soft popping noise sounded to our right, and we snapped our attention toward it. Frozen in place, we scanned the trees for any sign of what had made the sound. We heard a crunch, like something had taken a bite of an apple, and footsteps approached us, rustling the leaves.

"What is that?" Jaime whispered, freezing in place.

Before any of us could muster the courage to admit we didn't know, a raspy voice called out, "Who's there?"

I gulped and looked at Nolan in fear. Jaime clung to Cameron's arm, and Cameron placed his hand on Jaime's, huddling close to him.

"What do we do?" Jaime whispered.

The footsteps grew closer, and we remained in place, terrified to move. Soon after, a thin, bearded man came into view, a half-eaten apple in his left hand.

"What are you kids doing out here at night?" the man asked.

"Umm," I hesitated.

"We were just cutting through the orchard," Nolan gulped.

He nodded, accepting the explanation. "I wouldn't spend much time out in these trees if I were you," he replied.

"Why?" I couldn't help but ask.

"Never know what's out here," the man replied, scanning the trees.

"Especially at night," he added.

"What does that mean?" Jaime replied anxiously.

"Your mama never told you stories of what lives in these hills?" he asked.

I gulped. My mother had told me many stories of the things that lurked within the Appalachian Mountains. We'd even gone to see the Mothman statue in West Virginia one summer.

"Maybe we should go," I stammered to my friends, my hands starting to shake.

They nodded, and we carefully backed out of the woods, leaving the man to his own devices.

"What a creep," Nolan spat as we exited the orchard and began walking along the shoulder of the road.

"Do you think he was serious?" Jaime asked.

"He was just trying to scare us," Cameron assured him.

I wasn't so sure. Every few seconds I glanced at the tree line, hoping that nothing was staring back at me.

***

We finally arrived at the front door of the manor and stepped onto the creaky porch.

"You don't actually think it's unlocked, do you?" Nolan said as Cameron reached for the handle.

The handle emitted a metallic clang as the deadbolt prevented Cameron from pushing it open.

"Damn," Cameron whispered.

"Really would've been too easy," Jaime commented, and we looked around for another way in.

We approached the back of the building and peered up at the spiderwebs decorating the corner of a second-floor window.

"Odds of it being unlocked?" I wondered out loud.

Nolan contorted his lips as he thought and nodded, finally.

"I don't even know if windows this old can lock," he said.

"Give me a boost," Cameron instructed, handing his gear to Jaime to hold.

Jaime slung Cameron's backpack over his shoulder and cradled the camera and tripod in his arms.

"Oh man, I love this shirt," Jaime whined, as a screw from the tripod scraped a string out of the rose design in his red lace top.

Nolan and I cupped our hands and nodded at Cameron. He placed a hand on each of our shoulders and stepped into our hands, then we slowly lifted him, positioning him at the perfect height to inspect the window.

"I need to get a little closer," he whispered down to us.

Jaime watched from the side, checking over his shoulders every now and then to ensure we remained alone. Nolan and I scooted toward the mahogany beams and leaned our shoulders against them, the wood creaking as we did.

"That good?" Nolan grunted in Cameron's direction.

"Perfect," Cameron replied.

He placed his palms against the windowpane and pushed up. He applied a little bit more pressure, and the window slid open just enough that he could get his fingers underneath.

He pushed the window up and hoisted himself into it, using his elbows to hold on to the windowsill. Nolan and I guided his legs upward until we could no longer reach, and Cameron dove face-first into the room.

A few moments went by. Cameron had seemed to disappear. The three of us looked at each other and finally, Nolan called up to him, "You good?"

We listened intently for a response that didn't come. We debated what to do until Cameron appeared in the window. He held up his hand, tightly gripping the Phantaphone.

"Got it," he said, grinning.

I let out a sigh of relief, accompanied by a subtle laugh from Nolan.

Jaime passed the camera equipment up to Cameron.

Pulling the tripod inside, Cameron said, "meet me at the back door and I'll let you guys in."

We nodded and walked together to a black door at the back of the house. It sat above three moss-covered concrete steps and looked like it had been painted hundreds of times. In spots, you could even see the remnants of white paint where the black had chipped away.

"Oh, my god!" Jaime yelped, jumping from the top step onto the grass.

I instinctively grabbed Nolan's biceps, and he wrapped his free arm around me.

"What?" I whispered in a panic.

Jaime pointed to the top left corner of the door and we followed the invisible line from his finger to a large spider web.

A spider the size of a half-dollar clung to a strand of web in front of the door.

Nolan sighed and reached forward, collecting the spider in his hand, and carefully placed it in the grass near the manor's foundation. Jaime pinched his lips together in embarrassment and we laughed.

The black door swung into the kitchen, and Cameron stepped to the side, allowing us to enter.

"What's so funny?" he asked as we stepped inside.

"There was a spider and I may or may not have screamed like a child," Jaime poked fun at himself.

"Don't worry, Nolan saved him," I confirmed.

Nolan sighed, a look of mild annoyance on his face.

Jaime passed the camera equipment to Cameron, and he turned toward the atrium, the camera bag slung over one shoulder. We followed him to Martha's room.

Cameron wasted no time. He set up his infrared camera in the corner of the room so that it would capture anything that happened, then he handed an old still camera to me.

"Take pictures every few minutes and make sure you get multiple shots from each angle so we can compare," he instructed.

"What's that for?" Nolan asked, pointing to the camera.

Cameron looked annoyed by the question. "C'mon Nolan, everyone knows you're supposed to take still photos so you can rule out environmental factors like bugs, human movement, open windows, etc."

"Silly me," Nolan replied, holding up his hands defensively.

Jaime moved to the doorway and snapped a few pictures of the room, waiting for each to print before taking the next shot. Then, he pointed the camera at the mirror and clicked the shutter.

Cameron snatched the picture from Jaime as soon as he removed it from the printer and looked at it as Jaime snapped another.

"Are you guys seeing this?" Cameron asked excitedly.

We leaned over his shoulders and Jaime held the fresh print up next to the one Cameron was holding.

"That's the girl from my mirror!" I exclaimed.

A faint outline of a girl could be seen in the photo that Cameron was holding. Only the flash of the camera could be seen in Jaime's.

"Where is she?" Jaime asked, looking around the room.

Cameron flipped on the Phantaphone and yelled over the white noise, "Martha, can you show yourself?"

The sound of creaking wood echoed in from the hallway and the four of us turned toward it.

While Nolan, Jaime, and I remained frozen in fear, Cameron confidently moved toward the bedroom door and stepped into the hallway. The noise from the Phantaphone grew louder as it bounced off the walls around him.

"Is that you, Martha?" Cameron asked the empty hallway.

Footsteps sounded down the hall, and Cameron moved toward them in the direction of the main staircase.

Jaime and I clung to Nolan's arms as we took a step toward the hallway. The tall wooden door of Martha's bedroom slammed shut in front of us and we jumped back in fear.

Nolan tiptoed backward until his back was against the wall opposite the door, pulling Jaime and I into his chest. Our eyes were locked on the door.

Footsteps stomped down the hallway, and we braced ourselves for a confrontation as the doorknob shook violently.

"Guys!" Cameron yelled from the other side of the door. "Let me in!"

Nolan gently pushed away from Jaime and I and moved to the door. He placed his hand on the knob and attempted to turn it, but it didn't budge. He backed up and inspected the door, then flicked a small switch on the handle, unlocking it.

Cameron threw the door open in a panic and rushed inside.

"Not cool, dude!" Cameron scolded Nolan, out of breath.

"What?" Nolan asked, surprised.

"You locked me in the hallway alone!" Cameron exclaimed.

"I didn't touch it!" Nolan replied, "the lock must've engaged when the wind blew the door shut."

Cameron glared at him. "Oh, sure, the wind," he spat.

"What are you trying to say, dude?" Nolan asked.

"We all know you think I'm ridiculous for believing in ghosts," Cameron explained, gesturing toward Jaime and I as he said it.

"I didn't lock the door!" Nolan insisted.

Jaime chimed in, "he's telling the truth, none of us touched it."

I added, "the door closed all by itself."

The infrared camera clicked in the corner, and Cameron raced toward it.

"The battery died," he gasped, adding, "you guys saw me charge it. It was fully charged."

Footsteps creaked in the hallway once again and Cameron raced toward them, leaving the Phantaphone behind on the bedspread.

Jaime and I leaned into the hallway to watch as Cameron turned on the flashlight on his phone and shined it around the empty hallway. Nolan picked up the infrared camera and inspected it.

A sound, like tapping on glass, caused us to back into the room and turn toward the mirror just as the door slammed shut once again.

The lights in the room flicked on for just a brief moment, distracting us from the door. Martha stared back at us from inside the mirror, a worried expression on her face.

"Stay together," a soft whisper floated through the room as her lips moved.

The three of us exchanged glances as we watched Martha disappear, leaving only our reflections in the mirror.

"What the hell!" Jaime exclaimed in fear.

"Calm down." Nolan placed a hand on his shoulder.

"What does that mean?" I asked frantically as Jaime struggled to calm himself, pacing the room, his breath uneven.

Jaime suddenly froze. "Oh, my god! Cameron is alone!"

"Stay together," I repeated Martha's words.

"Shit," Nolan spat, as he lunged toward the door and flung it open.

A scream sounded from the floor above us and we followed closely behind Nolan as he ran toward the sound.

"Cameron?" Nolan yelled as we ran to the stairs.

Nolan bounded up the stairs and stopped running only when he reached the peach room.

He stepped inside and spoke hesitantly, "Cam?"

Jaime and I stepped so that we could see into the room around Nolan. Cameron stood in the center of the room, eyes glued to a portrait of Landon and Edith.

"Cam?" Nolan asked again.

Cameron didn't move. Jaime approached him cautiously and placed a hand on his cheek, guiding Cameron to look at him.

He turned to Jaime, a look of pure terror in his eyes.

"What happened?" Jaime asked.

Nolan and I stepped forward, urging him to respond. He slowly raised his arm and pointed at the portrait. We turned toward the painting, but saw nothing.

"It was there," Cameron whispered.

"What?" Jaime asked.

Cameron, still frozen in fear, replied, "the shadow."

"The one me and Nolan saw?" I asked.

Cameron nodded, slowly lowering his arm to his side.

He leaned down to collect pieces of the Phantaphone that were scattered across the floor.

"What happened to it?" Nolan asked, leaning down to help him.

"I dropped it," Cameron muttered.

"It's destroyed," he added with a sigh.

"We can make a new one," I offered sympathetically.

"The investigation is ruined," Cameron whined.

"No, it's not," Jaime comforted him.

Cameron sighed, "the camera is dead, the Phantaphone is broken..."

"We still have the still camera," Jaime said, holding up the camera.

"And the digital recorder," Nolan added, pulling the device from his pocket.

"Let's go back to Martha's room and see if we can talk to her," I suggested.

Cameron nodded and took Jaime's hand, rising to his feet.

The two of them led us back to Martha's room.

We stood in front of the mirror and Cameron immediately asked her for answers, "Martha, please just tell us what is going on."

The lights flickered just as they had before and slowly a figure appeared in the reflection, almost like a photo was being rendered. Her black hair, pale white skin and sporadic freckles were impossible to mistake.

We stared back at Martha until Cameron gained the courage to speak to her. "Can you please tell us what is going on?" he asked.

Martha seemed nervous, looking around the room without addressing Cameron's question.

"If you can't talk, you can use sign language," Cameron offered, "I learned it in high school."

"Really?" Nolan was surprised by Cameron's revelation.

"Yeah," Cameron confirmed.

I rested my hand on Nolan's bicep, as we waited for Martha to respond.

"Please," Cameron pleaded to her.

"We heard you talk before," Jaime encouraged her. "You told us to stay together, so here we are, together."

"You heard her talk?" Cameron asked, his eyes wide.

I nodded and Martha let a soft hiss escape her lips, urging us to be silent. Our mouths shut, and we focused our attention on her.

"We can't talk here. He'll hear us," she said.

The four of us looked at each other, not entirely sure what she meant. Her face began to fade away as it had earlier and I yelled in a whisper, "Wait! Where *can* we talk?"

"Take the mirror out of the manor and I'll explain," she replied. Then she was gone.

As we processed the interaction, a door creaked below us, followed by the flick of a light switch and the sound of soft footsteps.

Our eyes grew in their sockets.

Nolan whispered, "I think someone is here."

"Hello," a familiar voice called from the atrium.

"Shit, it's Ellie," Cameron hissed. "What do we do?"

"I'll take care of it," Jaime said, stepping toward the bedroom door. "I have a key to the manor. I'll tell her I just came to get a book from the study."

"You have a key!" I exclaimed in a whisper.

"I didn't bring it with me, obviously," he clarified.

"You can't make this up," Nolan sighed, rolling his eyes.

"Okay, you go distract Ellie," I said, "and we'll sneak out the back door."

"See if you can get her into the sitting room and give us a sign when the coast is clear," Nolan instructed Jaime.

He nodded. "Got it. I'll ask her about the orchard and get her over to the window, then I'll say 'it's a bit cold out tonight' and that will be your sign to leave," he replied.

"Perfect," I said.

Jaime exited the bedroom, and we listened as his footsteps descended the staircase.

Ellie yelped and Jaime said, "Oh my god, I'm so sorry. I didn't mean to scare you."

"What are you doing here with all the lights off?" she asked.

"I had a question at the asylum yesterday, so I figured I'd stop by and see if I could find the answer in the study," Jaime explained.

"With the lights off?" she asked with a nervous laugh.

"Yeah," Jaime laughed it off, "I just figured I'd run up real fast. I didn't bother turning the lights on. I wouldn't want to leave one on by accident."

She laughed, seeming to believe his story. "You're lucky you didn't fall," she said.

"Yeah, I should probably be more careful," he agreed.

"What brings *you* here?" he asked.

"I got a notification that the motion detector was set off on the third floor," she replied. "It must've been you."

"Yeah, sorry about that," Jaime laughed.

"Since you're here, maybe you could answer the question for me?" he said.

"Oh, of course," she replied. "What is it?"

The talking became more difficult to discern. Jaime must have led her away to the sitting room. Cameron lifted the mirror from the wall and tried to tuck it under his shoulder, struggling with the camera equipment already in his arms.

"Give it to me," Nolan whispered, snatching the mirror from him.

The three of us crept to the top of the staircase to listen for the signal phrase.

"Oh my," Jaime said, "it's a bit cold out tonight."

"Go," Nolan whispered, gesturing toward the stairs.

Cameron and I moved down the staircase as quietly as we could, Nolan following close behind. I peeked into the sitting room to see Ellie's and Jaime's backs to us and nodded to Nolan and Cameron.

The three of us lurked toward the kitchen as quickly as we could and carefully opened the back door. Nolan went out first, ducking into the shadow cast by the monstrous building. Cameron and I followed, quietly closing the door behind us.

We ran toward the orchard and paused when we were sure we couldn't be seen from the windows. Nolan ordered a ride on his phone and Cameron texted Jaime to let him know where we were.

When Jaime managed to free himself from the conversation with Ellie, he met up with us at the edge of the road.

After a short discussion, we decided it was best not to take the mirror into the car. Cameron agreed to stay back with Jaime and the mirror, while Nolan and I rode together back to his apartment.

We arrived at the apartment and waited for the driver to leave. Then we got in Nolan's car and drove to retrieve our friends.

Chapter 16

Back at Nolan's apartment, we propped the mirror against the wall outside Nolan's bedroom, and Cameron plugged his infrared camera into the wall. He set it up on a tripod in the corner of the room, determined to catch Martha on camera.

When Cameron was satisfied with his setup, the four of us stood in front of the mirror.

"Martha, are you here?" Cameron asked.

We waited a few moments, and she appeared, just as she had before.

"Can you tell us what is going on?" Nolan asked her.

She nodded and looked around the room one last time before speaking.

"There is a dark entity at the manor," she explained.

"Who?" Cameron asked impatiently.

Martha glared at him.

"Let her talk," I scolded Cameron.

"My father has taken control of the manor," she continued, "I believe he is coming for you too."

She looked at Nolan, and he pointed to himself.

"Because I'm related to Reginald?" he asked.

"You know him?" Martha perked up.

"No," Nolan replied, and her face fell.

"But apparently I'm related to him," Nolan added.

Martha thought for a moment, and Jaime chimed in. "Did Landon kill Reginald?"

Martha nodded.

"How did he do it?" Cameron asked, intrigued.

Martha glared at him, and I swatted his bicep.

"This is why spirits don't talk to you," I lectured him.

"Sorry," Cameron shrugged.

"What do you want with us?" I asked her. "Why do you keep contacting me?"

Martha looked at the ground and breathed. "I was hoping you'd find him for me."

"Reginald?" Nolan asked.

She nodded.

"We did!" Cameron exclaimed.

Martha perked up, but before she could reply, I interjected, "Why me? Why us?"

Her expression soft, she replied, "I saw the two of you in the mirror." She looked at Nolan, "you reminded me of my aunt and uncle, so in love..." she trailed off.

Nolan and I exchanged glances.

"We weren't even dating yet," I said.

Ignoring us, she turned to Cameron. "Where? Where did you see him?"

"His grave is next to the railroad tracks in the orchard," Cameron explained, adding, "he led me there."

Martha looked as if she might cry. *Can ghosts cry?* I wondered.

"You really didn't know?" I asked, a sadness in my voice.

"I knew he was gone," she explained, "I just knew in my heart he was gone."

She sniffled. "I went into the orchard to search for him," she started to explain.

Cameron interrupted her, "Is that how you got sick?"

"Sick?" she replied, confusion in her voice.

"Tuberculosis," Jaime clarified, in an attempt to jog her memory.

"I didn't die from Tuberculosis!" she barked, her voice deep and commanding, causing us to jump. "I hung myself from the posts of my father's bed!"

We gasped collectively and Jaime covered his mouth with his hands, tears forming in his eyes.

"Oh my god, I'm so sorry," Jaime said, "I had no idea."

"I believe my father is preventing me from contacting Uncle Reginald in the afterlife," she explained.

"What do you mean?" I asked.

"Every time I try to speak, my voice gets drowned out," Martha replied. "I think he's doing something to stop me from talking. Can you find a way to stop him? Can you find a way to help me say goodbye to Uncle Reginald?"

"So that's why you couldn't talk to us in the manor?" Nolan asked.

She nodded. "I didn't want him to hurt you if he found out that I could talk to you in the mirror."

Nolan turned to the cracked Cameron had fixed on the wall behind us, the spot still slightly sunken in.

"If your father is the one behind all of this, I don't think we're safe here," he said.

Martha looked at the crack and her eyes went wide.

"He did that?" she asked.

I nodded, then she disappeared.

Chapter 17

We decided to reconvene in the morning once we'd all had time to process our trip to the manor. Cameron and Jaime left for the night, and Nolan and I retired to his room. Nolan laid on his back, his black V-neck shirt providing a soft pillow for my head as I listened to his heartbeat.

"Goodnight, Zoey," he whispered as I closed my eyes.

***

The sound of glass shattering yanked me from my slumber and I jolted into a seated position. Nolan jumped too, balancing himself on his elbows, he whispered, "What was that?"

"I don't know," I cautiously replied, my eyes refusing to leave the bedroom door knob terrified someone might open it.

Footsteps travelled down the hallway, approaching the other side of the door painfully slowly. I yearned to find comfort in Nolan's arms, but I couldn't bring myself to move. The fear shot through my veins and a cold sensation overtook my extremities. The footsteps halted outside the door.

All we could hear was the shaky breaths of air leaving our lungs.

Our eyes glued to the door handle, we waited like prey for whatever lurked on the other side to strike.

As minutes passed, I mustered the courage to inch my way toward Nolan's chest. We wrapped our arms around each other without letting the door leave our sight.

The room grew colder and silence blanketed the room as our breaths caught in our throats.

The blankets flew from the bed, exposing our legs. They hit the wall and fell in a pile, blocking the light coming in underneath the door and hindering our exit.

I looked toward the window and wondered if it was a suitable escape route as the door knob violently shook.

Nolan pulled me tighter to his chest, both arms wrapped around my body protectively, his breathing erratic.

A grey figure materialized above us, its familiar glowing eyes peering into my own. Wind blew through the open window to our right, flapping the curtain just enough to let some moon light in. The figure appeared to fade each time darkness blanketed the room.

Neither of us moved as the figure hovered above the bed. Nolan adjusted his body, so that he was in between the figure and myself.

"What do you want?" he bravely, although shakily asked.

The yellow orbs on what seemed to be its face went dark as if the figure had closed its eyes. It became invisible, masked by the darkness as the curtains stilled.

Nolan loosened his grip on me, looking around the room in a panic as if to find where the figure had gone.

Suddenly, the curtains flew to the side, moonlight invading the room.

A cold skeleton-like hand wrapped around each of my ankles and swiftly pulled. Without enough time to place my hands, my back connected with the mattress and I was violently pulled toward the end of the bed.

My body turned, as if I was being swung like a bat. The grip on my ankles released, and my head connected with the wall behind me. Sheetrock crumbled to the floor at my sides and I was thankful to be conscious.

Nolan sprung from the bed and lunged toward me.

"Don't touch her!" he screamed at the shadow.

He reached for my hand to pull me to my feet, but as our fingers met Nolan let out a cry of agony. His left hand moved to wrap around his right and he bent over in pain. He lifted his hand to reveal a fresh scrape across the length of his forearm.

I turned my head to the figure, a look of pure terror on my face.

"What do you want from us?" I cried out in its direction.

The figure seemed to darken as it breathed in an eerie hiss of air.

"Stay away," it bellowed.

"From what?" Nolan shouted at the figure.

A clatter sounded from the living room. Nolan jumped from the bed and kicked the blankets out the way before throwing the bedroom door open. I scooted backward along the floor, away from the figure, watching it carefully. I scooted out of the room, then jumped to my feet. I ran to Nolan, clutching his bicep. He stood in the hallway staring at the mirror, face up on the carpet, shattered.

"No," I whispered to myself.

I turned to find the shadow, now more like a man, with discernable Victorian attire and slicked back hair. A devious smile came over its face, now with discernible features, including a well-groomed mustache, identical to the one in the manor's portrait. I tightened my grip on Nolan's arm as we faced Mr. Meridion.

"Landon," Nolan addressed the figure. "What do you want from us?"

The man turned his head to the right and looked at the mirror, a sinister smile still plastered across his face.

I picked up a lamp from the side table and launched it at the man.

"Let her go!" I screamed, the strain of the throw making my voice more of a growl.

The figure disappeared in an instant and the lamp crashed into the bay window at the front of the apartment. The bulb let out an echoing pop as it shattered to the floor. We stood, unmoving, for a moment, allowing our breaths to steady.

Nolan turned to me and asked, "Are you okay?"

I nodded, and he moved to the front door, flicking the light switch to illuminate the room. Pieces of the lamp scattered across the floor at the front of the apartment and shards from the mirror stuck out from the carpet fibers.

We both stared at the mess processing what had happened. As we tried to gather our thoughts, a frantic knock came at the door. Nolan looked at the clock on the wall, just after one in the morning, and shot me a confused look, as if to ask, "Who is that?"

He took a few steps and unlocked the door. Mr. Stevens barged through the door as soon as the lock clicked loose.

"What the hell was that noise?" he barked, looking around the apartment.

He glanced at the broken mirror and studied the lamp on the carpet. Then, he turned to Nolan with an angry glare.

"I have no tolerance for wife beaters!" Mr. Stevens yelled.

Nolan opened his mouth to respond, but Mr. Stevens stepped toward him and added, "you wanna throw things at someone, throw it at me and see where that gets ya!"

"I didn't throw anything!" Nolan yelled back.

Before Mr. Stevens could respond I chimed in, "I threw the lamp."

The landlord's expression softened as much as a grumpy old man's could, and he turned to me. A faint laugh escaped his lips and he looked back at Nolan, his eyes narrowing.

"What'd you do to deserve it?" he barked.

"It was the spirit," I explained.

Mr. Stevens laughed, genuinely this time. "The ghost did it! You think I haven't heard that one before?"

Nolan sighed, and I replied, "we have it on camera, we'll prove it."

The landlord laughed once more, seemingly amused by the game he believed Nolan was playing.

"I'll tell you what," he said with a grin. "You show me a video of a ghost in this apartment, a real ghost," he clarified, "and I'll renew your lease."

Nolan looked at me, somewhat nervously, like he didn't know what to say.

"Deal!" I replied for him.

Mr. Stevens moved toward the door, still laughing. As he stepped onto the sidewalk, he barked, "you have until the thirtieth," then he pulled the door shut behind him.

"Great," Nolan said, throwing his hands up.

I moved toward him and placed a hand on his shoulder.

"This is good," I said, encouragingly, "we just need to get Cameron over here with the camera and then you don't have to worry about moving."

He let the air out of his lungs and raised his eyebrows.

"Yeah, I guess," he muttered.

We quickly cleaned up the mess and returned to Nolan's bedroom in hopes of getting at least a little bit of sleep before the sun came up.

***

When the sun creeped through the curtains the following morning, I kissed Nolan on the cheek and reached for my phone on the nightstand and texted Cameron.

Zoey: Hey, you busy after work today?

I set my phone on the blankets beside me and rolled to cuddle into Nolan's chest. He sleepily lifted his arm to give me access and rested it on my back.

"Good morning," he groggily mumbled.

I lifted my chin and placed a soft kiss on his lips in response.

We laid in silence, allowing our bodies to adjust to the morning.

When my phone buzzed, I rolled over to read the message.

Cameron: Going to dinner with Jaime. Why?

My face fell in disappointment and I turned my body so Nolan wouldn't see the messages.

Zoey: I was going to ask if you wanted to do a ghost hunt in Nolan's apartment.

Zoey: Maybe tomorrow?

He replied almost immediately.

Cameron: We could stop by after dinner!

Zoey: Perfect!

I smiled in satisfaction and set my phone on the nightstand before turning back to Nolan.

"What?" he asked, still half asleep.

"Cameron is going to bring the camera over tonight," I spoke with a grin.

He nodded in response.

I perked up, sitting cross-legged, facing Nolan.

"What do you want for breakfast?" I asked.

He thought for a moment.

"Surprise me," he said.

I went to the kitchen and began locating the ingredients for one of my favorite dishes, Finnish pancakes, a recipe I'd learned from an exchange student in college.

When the oven finished preheating, I placed the glass dish inside and set a timer on my phone. Then I returned to Nolan's room to change. Nolan was pulling a shirt on as I entered.

"Last night was real, right?" he asked, with skepticism in his voice. "It wasn't a dream?"

I nodded as I pulled a pair of shorts on. "Yeah," I breathed, finding it hard to believe myself.

"There was a ghost." Nolan stated, as if he was trying to convince himself. "In my room," he added.

I nodded once more and walked toward him, lifting my arms to wrap them around his neck. He placed his hand on my hips and pulled me close, then wrapped them around me in a warm embrace.

"Yeah, there was a ghost," I confirmed.

He quietly held me, then whispered, "I love you, Zoey."

I smiled up at him and said, "I love you too, Nolan."

We moved to the kitchen and Nolan helped set the table for breakfast as we waited for the food to finish baking. When the timer went off, I put an oven mitt on and removed the glass dish, setting it on top of the stove.

"Smells good," Nolan said, leaning over my shoulder to see what I'd made.

I turned to find a look of confusion on his face and laughed.

"It's Finnish pancakes," I said, "it tastes like French toast, but it looks like Yorkshire pudding."

He nodded. "Sounds good to me."

I pulled open a drawer next to the stove and grabbed a spatula. Then I carried the dish to the table and set it on a towel Nolan had laid on the table.

We ate together, and then Nolan dropped me off at my apartment on his way to work.

"I'll see you tonight." I said, before closing the car door and watching him drive away.

I entered my apartment and showered, then changed into a work-appropriate outfit, a tight-fitting black t-shirt and black pants. I stared into the bathroom mirror as I wrangled my hair into a loose bun, allowing a strand to hang loose on either side of my face.

Part of me hoped Martha would replace my reflection. There was a chance she had some insight into our encounter last night, and I longed to ask her about it.

"Martha?" I whispered. Feeling a bit foolish as I spoke to my own reflection.

I closed my eyes and sighed when she didn't appear, then picked up a makeup brush and my favorite palette of eye-shadow. Brushing the powder over my eyelids, I kept an eye on the mirror in hopes that she'd appear. When I finished my makeup, I pursed my lips in disappointment and opened my phone to order a ride to work.

***

When my shift ended, Cameron and I hung out aprons on hooks next to the backdoor of the restaurant.

"You want a ride home?" Cameron asked.

When I hesitated, he added, "we're driving right past your apartment."

"There aren't any restaurants over there," I challenged him.

A smile exploded across his face. "We're not going to a restaurant," he said.

"Where are you going, then?" I asked.

"We're going to Jaime's parent's house!" he gushed.

My lower jaw fell open in excitement. "Wait! You and Jaime are dating? Like, officially?"

"Yeah," he gushed, "I'm meeting them for the first time. Jaime says they're really excited to meet me!"

"That's so exciting!" I replied, happy for my friend.

"I know!" he said. "I've been waiting to tell you all night, I could barely hold it in."

"What are you wearing?" I asked, a hint of concern in my voice as I looked at his grease-stained black t-shirt.

He pulled a rainbow Hawaiian shirt out of his backpack and held it up for me to see.

"That's a bit on the head, don't you think?" I asked.

"Jaime has two moms," Cameron replied. "I thought it'd be a good icebreaker."

I shrugged. "Well, in that case, I think it's perfect."

He smiled in response and turned toward the bathrooms, located just beyond the swinging door behind me.

"I'm going to change real quick and I'll meet you in my car," he said, tossing me the keys.

As he pushed through the doors, he turned to wink.

"Don't leave without me," he teased.

"I would never," I assured him with a playful eye roll.

He disappeared into the bathroom, and I wandered toward the parking lot to find his car. I unlocked the passenger door and sat to wait for him.

As I waited, I opened the photo app on my phone and found the picture of Nolan and I from the night we met at the manor. It seemed like so long ago now.

I thought back on how adamant I'd been that I wasn't interested in a relationship at the time. It seemed foolish now considering all we'd been through together and how much I missed him after only being apart for a mere ten hours.

Zoey: Dinner at my place tonight? I make a great Alfredo sauce.

I set my phone in my lap and smiled, contently. It was hard to even recall the last time I'd had a boyfriend. I had to admit, it was kind of nice to feel wanted.

My phone buzzed in my lap, and I picked it up.

Nolan: Sounds good to me!

I smiled at my phone as Cameron opened the driver's side door. He grinned at me mischievously as he sat down and pulled the door shut.

"What?" I asked, defensively.

"You're smiling at your phone like a teenage boy with a porn magazine," he replied.

"Speaking from experience?" I raised an eyebrow as I teased him.

"Maybe," he replied, smugly.

I rolled my eyes, but I couldn't hold it in any longer. A smile came over my lips and I said, "okay, you can't repeat this."

"What?" he asked, turning his body toward me, anticipation in his voice.

"Nolan told me he loves me last night," I beamed.

Cameron's jaw dropped, "Oh my gosh!"

"I know, right?" I replied.

"You said it back, right?" he asked.

"Obviously," I replied.

He placed a hand on his heart. "I cannot wait to be your best man."

I laughed. "Woah, let's not get ahead of ourselves, Cam."

He smiled, turning toward the windshield and putting the car in drive. "Cameron Flint, matchmaker extraordinaire," he cockily announced.

As we pulled into the parking lot of my apartment complex, Cameron turned to me, a serious look on his face.

"Please don't say anything to Nolan about me and Jaime," he said.

"Okay," I replied. "You aren't telling him?"

"I just don't know how he'll react," Cameron said shyly.

"I'm sure he'll be happy for you," I responded.

"I'm just not ready to tell him," he admitted.

"Okay, I won't say anything," I promised.

***

"How was dinner?" I asked cautiously as Cameron and Jaime settled into Nolan's couch.

Jaime and Cameron looked at each other as if they were trying to decide who should speak.

Cameron shrugged and turned to me.

"Good, Jaime's moms were really cool," he replied, after checking to make sure Nolan's door was still shut.

"My moms loved him!" Jaime raved.

The conversation was cut short when Nolan emerged from the bedroom.

Jaime looked at Nolan and I as if he was expecting something. Nolan raised an eyebrow at me, and I smiled innocently.

"I may have told Cameron about us," I admitted.

"And I may have told Jaime," Cameron added.

Nolan nodded, a smile creeping onto his face. Before he could speak, Cameron clapped his hands together. "So, how about that ghost hunt?"

Nolan scoffed.

"What's your problem?" Cameron asked.

"Long story short, Landon Meridion visited us last night," I replied.

Cameron's eyes went wide, as did Jaime's. "You saw him again?"

Nolan and I looked at each other and sighed together. Then Nolan relayed to them the events of the night before.

"No way!" Cameron gasped, excitement in his eyes.

"We have to get him on camera, though, or Mr. Stevens is going to evict Nolan," I explained.

"So you guys want to summon an evil spirit back to the apartment?" Jaime clarified, hesitantly.

"We have to prove to him that the damage is being caused by supernatural entities," I said.

"You realize there are like a ton of other apartments to choose from, right?" Jaime asked, looking at Nolan like he wanted to check him into the asylum next time he went to work.

"I like this apartment," Nolan replied. "Plus, Mr. Stevens owns most of the complexes in town."

"He owns my complex," I said.

"Let's get this asshole on camera," he said, holding up his fully charged infrared camera.

Nolan flicked off the lights and the three of us huddled behind Cameron as he walked toward the mirror, which was leaning against the wall just outside the bathroom. We peered over his shoulder to watch the small LCD screen.

"Landon," I said softly, "Can you show yourself?"

Cameron stopped walking and lowered the camera to his hip as he turned to glare at me.

"You don't just nicely ask an evil spirit to show itself," he scoffed.

"What am I supposed to do?" I replied defensively, in a whisper.

He rolled his eyes, seemingly annoyed that I wasn't familiar with the best practices of communicating with spirits.

"Watch and learn," he replied, lifting the camera back to his eye level.

"You want to break things?" Cameron bellowed. "I bet you can't break something right now."

"Don't encourage it!" Nolan said, annoyed.

"Do you want it on camera or not?" Cameron asked.

Nolan sighed.

"C'mon, break something," Cameron barked toward the hallway. "Or are you too weak?"

Jaime gripped the back of Cameron's Hawaiian shirt in fear as we walked a few more steps. We reached the mirror and turned to face it, the camera lens pointing directly at the shattered glass.

"Did you do this?" Cameron asked.

The hallway light flickered above us, and Cameron looked up at it.

"Is that you?" he asked, "Who are you?"

Jaime huddled close to us and whispered, "I don't think this is a good idea."

Cameron pulled a rectangular device out of his pocket and handed it to Jaime, who inspected it.

"It's an EMF detector," Cameron explained, "it searches for electromagnetic energy, which ghosts are said to give off. If you see a spike, it means something is here with us."

The lights flickered above us again, and Jaime dropped the EMF detector.

"It's moving," he said fearfully.

Nolan leaned down to retrieve the device from the floor and we watched the needle move to the right, indicating an increase in electromagnetic energy.

"Show yourself!" Nolan yelled.

We all heard what sounded like a voice coming from down the hall and turned toward it.

"Did you say something," Cameron asked, hoping the ghost would respond.

A chill came over the apartment and we moved closer to each other. Nolan placed his hand protectively around my waist.

The muffled voice came again.

"What is it saying?" Jaime asked.

"I don't know," Cameron replied.

"I have an idea," I said, taking the camera from Cameron and navigating to the playback screen.

"What are you doing?" Nolan asked.

"I'm trying to see if the camera captured the voice," I replied. "I've been doing some research. Ghost voices..."

Cameron interrupted me, "they're called EVPs, electronic voice phenomenon."

"EVPs," I corrected myself, glaring at Cameron, "can be heard through devices like digital recorders and cameras, even when the human ear can't pick them up."

I clicked on the most recent recording, and fast forwarded it to the end, then hit play.

We listened, holding our breath to ensure the apartment was silent. A whisper came through the camera speaker.

"Wait, what was that?" Jaime asked, gripping Cameron's arm.

Cameron took the camera from me and increased the volume, then he played the video again. We all leaned toward the camera to hear better.

The whisper came through again, clearer this time.

"Stay away!" Nolan exclaimed.

"That's the same thing it said last night," I explained to Cameron and Jaime.

Cameron's jaw dropped open. "Wait! Isn't that what the Ouija board said too?"

Nolan and I looked at each other, stunned.

"You're right!" I replied.

"So it was Landon all along?" Nolan asked rhetorically.

"Maybe he knows you're related to Reginald," I offered.

"Or maybe he knew you guys were contacting Martha," Jaime suggested.

"But Landon has never come to my apartment," I replied, "at least, not that I know of."

"Didn't your apartment get trashed, too?" Cameron asked me.

"You're right, I forgot about that," I replied.

"Does it really matter?" Nolan asked.

Cameron glared at him. "Of course it matters, we have to know why he's contacting us if we want to help him."

"Why would we want to help him?" Nolan snorted.

"He's a lost soul," Cameron snapped.

"He's an asshole," Nolan replied.

"Well, he's not going to leave you alone unless we figure out what he wants." Cameron shrugged.

"Maybe Edith can tell us," Jaime suggested, adding, "her mirror is at the asylum, it's how I've always talked to her."

"Good idea!" I replied.

"Can we show this to Mr. Stevens first, so I don't have to go find a new apartment?" Nolan said, pointing to the camera.

Cameron nodded, and we walked together to the leasing office at the far end of the building.

Mr. Stevens looked up from the monitor in front of him as we walked through the glass door across from him.

"Caught your ghost already?" he teased.

"In fact, we have," Nolan replied rudely.

He laughed. "Let's see it."

Cameron excitedly pulled up the video and handed the camera to Mr. Stevens.

"Just push play," he said with a grin.

Mr. Stevens raised an eyebrow skeptically, and we watched his expression intently as the voice came through.

He burst out laughing.

Nolan sighed. He could tell that Mr. Stevens wasn't buying it.

"Which one of your little friends did you get to whisper into the camera," Mr. Stevens asked in amusement.

"It's real," Cameron insisted.

"Come back when you have some real evidence," Mr. Stevens said, tossing the camera at Nolan.

Our shoulders dropped, and we sulked back to Nolan's apartment.

I rubbed his shoulder as he leaned over to unlock the door. "We'll prove it to him, " I assured him."

Chapter 18

The four of us met at O'Connell's when Cameron and I's shift ended on Friday night. The sun was beginning to set on the horizon as we piled into Jaime's car.

He'd insisted on driving, reasoning that his car would look the least suspicious at the asylum late at night.

"I have it all taken care of," Jaime assured us as we rode toward the asylum. "I put a midnight ghost tour on the schedule for tonight and assigned myself as the guide. Midnight tours are always private, so we should be the only one's here."

"Smart thinking," I replied.

"Couldn't that get you fired?" Nolan asked, concerned.

Jaime shot him a sly grin through the rearview mirror.

"Only if I get caught," he snarked.

"My motto!" Cameron laughed, "it's only illegal if you get caught."

I shook my head and sighed.

"It's all fun and games until you do finally get caught," I replied.

"I'm a professional," Cameron answered, with a hint of sass.

"What's the plan when we get there?" Nolan asked, changing the subject.

"I'll go in first, just to make sure we're alone," Jaime explained. "Then, we'll go up to Edith's room and see if we can get her to appear in the mirror. When she does, we'll ask her if she has any insight into what's going on."

***

We watched from the car as Jaime approached the main entrance. He wiggled his key into the lock and pushed the door open before disappearing inside the castle-like structure.

Nolan and I leaned forward in the backseat, our cheeks nearly touching, to get a better view out the windshield.

After what seemed like hours, but in reality was only a few minutes, Jaime's head poked out of the doorway and he used his hand to usher us inside.

We stepped out of the car and hurriedly walked toward the door Jaime was holding open, peeking over our shoulders every now and then to make sure we weren't being watched.

The familiar smell of mildew and the crack of debris being stepped on assured us we were safe inside the build.

Cameron stared up at the ceiling in awe and I noted that one of the loose banisters had fallen to the floor.

"This way," Jaime whispered, motioning for us to follow him up the stairs.

Cameron tripped over a loose tile and Jaime opened the flashlight app on his phone.

"Careful, there's a lot of loose debris," he said.

"Gee, thanks for the heads up," Cameron sarcastically replied.

I snickered as we followed Jaime to the west wing.

"This is it," Jaime announced in a whisper, stopping in front of Edith's room.

"Wow," Cameron whispered, taking in the room.

He moved inside and picked up the glass sitting on the side table. Inspecting it he said, "Did she actually drink out of this?"

We looked at Jaime, and he shrugged. "No clue. If I had to guess, it's probably just a prop."

Nolan and I approached the wall where the mirror hung.

Jaime stood beside us and explained, "last time I used a spell to get her to appear." Looking a bit embarrassed, he admitted, "I didn't know you could just ask her to show herself."

Cameron sighed.. "You all have so much to learn about the paranormal."

"Show us how it's done then," Jaime retorted.

"I will," Cameron asserted, stepping between us and the mirror.

"Edith, we'd like to talk to you," he said into the mirror.

Nothing happened. The only thing that could be seen in the mirror were our own faces staring back at us.

"Edith, it's me, Jaime. Can you come talk to me?" Jaime said.

The faint outline of a woman appeared in the mirror and Jaime playfully stuck his tongue out at Cameron, who returned the gesture.

"Edith?" I asked.

The outline disappeared.

"It's okay," Jaime said, "we just want to talk to you."

The image of Edith Meridion slowly reappeared in the mirror.

"Hi," Jaime said shyly.

She seemed nervous, moving only her eyes as she looked at each of us. Her lips were held in a straight line.

"We were just wondering if you could tell us more about Martha," I explained.

Her expression softened.

"Martha visited us, but her mirror broke, so we can't talk to her anymore," Jaime added.

"We were hoping you know how we can help her," I said. "She wants to contact Reginald."

Silence followed, and it was starting to seem like we weren't going to get anywhere with Edith. Then she let her mouth open, just enough for a few words to escape.

"Martha is speaking with you?" she asked, a crack in her voice.

"Yes," Jaime confirmed.

"We think Landon is stopping Martha from contacting Reginald," I explained, "but we don't know how to help her."

Edith maintained an emotionless expression. Even in death, it was clear that her years in the asylum had taken a toll on her.

Nolan stepped forward and asked, "Do you know what happened to Reginald?"

Edith's expression changed for the first time, a look of sorrow came across her face. Her eyes closed, and she looked like she could cry.

"My Reggie," she said, then sniffled.

"Did Landon have him killed?" Cameron asked.

She sniffled once more. It clearly pained her to think about it.

She brushed the thought away and straightened her head, "Landon killed him," she barked.

The four of us took a nervous step back from the mirror, and her face softened.

"Maybe Martha wants to get revenge on Landon for killing her uncle," Jaime suggested.

"I would want revenge if I were her," I agreed.

Nolan raised an eyebrow at me, and I shrugged. "Revenge is good therapy."

"Don't mess with her," Cameron jokingly whispered.

Jaime pulled us back to the conversation at hand, by saying, "guys, focus."

Edith spoke then, and we all jumped a bit, having almost forgotten she was part of the conversation. Her voice was once again soft and song-like, "my Martha would not harm anyone."

Cameron opened his mouth to speak, but Edith spoke over him, "when Reginald and Martha grew close, Landon grew nervous that he'd tell her the truth," she continued. "I suggested we banish him from the manor as a precaution, but Landon wouldn't have it."

"Then, Reginald gave her that mirror," she said, and a ghastly sigh echoed through the room and she revealed, "he beat the mirror with a chair and destroyed it."

We waited for her to continue and she said, "Reginald shoved him across the room and poor Martha cried."

It was clear that retelling the story pained her. She continued, "they made their way to the orchard and Martha followed them. I swear I tried to stop her," she said.

"What happened then?" I asked.

"He killed them both," Edith wailed.

The four of us looked at each other in horror.

"He..." Cameron hesitated, and it was one of the few times I'd seen Cameron speechless.

"He killed Martha?" Nolan finished the question for him.

Edith's face fell, and she explained, "of course I shouldn't be saying such things, I didn't see it."

The four of us exchanged glances, growing more and more confused as the conversation went on.

"So, you don't know for a fact that he killed them?" I clarified, confusion in my tone.

"Of course he did!" she bellowed, and I flinched at her words.

"That's why he sent me away. To this place." She lifted her arms and gestured toward the room.

"I thought he sent you here because you were seeing ghosts?" Jaime asked.

"He sent me here because he caught me speaking to my sister through the mirror in Martha's room. He heard me tell her I would go to the police," Edith explained.

She continued, "he never believed in the afterlife."

"But, you did?" I asked, hoping she'd say more.

She nodded. "My sister and I were very much involved in witchcraft, as some would call it," she replied.

"So, you are a psychic?" Cameron asked, wide-eyed.

Edith raised an eyebrow, seeming to be growing annoyed by him.

"From what I've learned about your family, Landon seems like too smart of a man to risk murder charges," Jaime commented.

"Reginald threatened to go to the press if Landon wouldn't tell Martha the truth," Edith explained. "It would've destroyed the Meridion name, everything Landon had worked so hard for."

"But why would he kill Martha?" I asked.

"Only he could tell you that," Edith replied.

"If she followed him into the orchard, she must've seen him kill Reginald," I guessed.

"So, you think he killed Martha because she was a witness?" Cameron asked, and I nodded.

Nolan, who'd been quiet throughout the conversation, huffed as if he'd just realized something. We watched as he nodded to himself.

"Wait," Nolan said, "Reginald Bauer married your sister, so that means Perida Bauer is your..."

She cut him off with a hint of a smile and confirmed, "my niece."

"How'd you know that?" Cameron asked Nolan.

Nolan shrugged, "I've been reading up on the history of the manor during my free period."

"Perida was the only one that visited me here," she said, nostalgically glancing around the room.

"Perida was the only one that believed me," she added.

"I taught her about the mirror and in exchange, she brought me things, like pastries." She smiled at the thought.

"You must have felt so alone here," I offered, looking around the room.

"Yes," she began. "Well, the visits from Perida made it more tolerable, I suppose."

"Did she visit you after you died?" I wondered.

"She did," Edith replied.

She continued, "when Perida passed away, she chose to move on to the afterlife. After that, Luisa visited for a while, then her daughter..." she trailed off.

"Lady Perida knows about the mirrors then," Cameron stated.

"Why didn't she tell us?" I asked, a little offended.

"Focus," Nolan said. "It's going to be morning by the time we're done here at this rate."

Jaime nodded, turning to Edith. "When was the last time you saw Luisa?"

"She told me that she had discovered Reginald's grave," Edith replied. "But she wouldn't bring me the watch so that I could speak with him."

"Why not?" Jaime asked.

"She wouldn't say," Edith replied. "I thought I'd never speak to him again."

She looked at me. "Until you showed up."

"Me?" I questioned. "What did I do?"

"You tell me," she replied with a snort. "Luisa visited me not long ago and informed me that Landon's spirit had grown restless again, thanks to a young girl."

"But," I defended myself. "Martha contacted me. I never tried to summon her or anything."

"Landon contacted us too," Nolan stated, "we didn't summon him either."

"You've spoken to my Martha?" Edith asked, and I nodded.

"You have to help her," Edith pleaded.

"Help her? How?" I asked. "The mirror is broken."

"Have the mirror fixed. Luisa can help. Then, bring it here," she said. "Maybe knowing the truth will help her move on," she added.

"How do you know Landon won't just come here and break it?" Nolan asked, adding, "he broke it in my apartment, not the manor."

"He has no connection to this place," she said sternly.

I opened my mouth to respond, but the only thing left was my reflection in the mirror.

"She's gone," Jaime confirmed.

"You don't say," Cameron replied, earning a glare from Jaime.

"What do we do now?" I asked.

"Get the mirror fixed," Nolan replied.

***

As we walked out of the room, Jaime stopped in the middle of the hallway.

"Wait, I want to show Cam the lobotomy room," he said, "he'll love it."

"Okay," I said with a shrug.

"We'll meet you in the atrium?" Nolan asked.

"Sounds good," Jaime smiled.

Nolan and I talked while we waited in the atrium.

"Are you okay?" Nolan asked.

"Yeah," I replied solemnly. "Edith just reminds me of my mom."

"How so?" he inquired.

"She couldn't be with the person she loved. Reminds me of how my dad left my mom," I replied, "and she died when her daughter was young, just like my mom."

Nolan nodded, then commented on Jaime and Cameron's absence, "They've been up there for a while. Do you think they're okay?"

"Maybe we should go check on them," I agreed.

A clatter sounded from above and Nolan took off running toward the west wing. Halfway up the stairs he turned to me and said, "Stay here!"

I watched nervously as he disappeared down the hallway, quickly becoming aware of how eerie the building was at night.

A loud gasp echoed from above, followed by Nolan's voice, "I'm sorry!"

"Nolan?" I called up the stairs.

He appeared soon after and descended the staircase, laughing.

I raised an eyebrow. "What happened?"

"Did you know Cameron and Jaime were a thing?" he asked, amused.

"Uhh," I replied, not wanting to give anything away.

"I just walked in on them making out in the lobotomy room," he clarified.

I let out a laugh. "I guess that explains why they were taking so long."

Jaime and Cameron rushed down the stairs, seemingly embarrassed.

"So, you finally found someone crazy enough to date you," Nolan teased Cameron.

Cameron tried to hold back a smile.

"He asked for my number after the Halloween party," Jaime said.

"That's great," Nolan replied, "I'm so happy for you two!"

Cameron's eyes lit up, and he gushed, "Thanks!"

"Did he offer you the Cameron special?" I teased Jaime. We all laughed.

"I didn't know how you'd respond to me dating another guy," Cameron admitted to Nolan.

Nolan looked offended. "Of course I support you!"

"So, when is our first double date?" Jaime asked with a grin.

"How about this weekend?" I replied.

Cameron and Nolan shrugged.

"Perfect," Jaime beamed.

Chapter 19

"How does one repair a magic mirror?" Nolan asked as we drove back to town.

"It's not a magic mirror," Cameron said with an eye roll, "it's paranormal equipment."

Nolan huffed, "whatever. How do we get it fixed?"

"Edith said Lady Perida could help," I said cautiously.

"Because she's been so much help in the past," Nolan snorted sarcastically.

"We're not asking her to get involved," I offered, "we're just asking her for advice."

"Nolan's right," Jaime responded. "She basically said she wouldn't help us at all."

"The worst she can say is no, right?" I replied. "I think we should give it a try."

"It's not like we know another psychic," Cameron added.

"You guys can go by yourselves then," Nolan scoffed. "I don't want anything to do with her."

"But she's your family," I encouraged him.

"Yeah, well, I don't talk to my dad," Nolan retorted, "and he's my family too."

I sighed in defeat.

"Just come with us," Cameron begged, "you don't have to talk to her."

"What's the point in me sitting there?" Nolan protested.

"I think she's more likely to help family than a group of random kids from town," I encouraged him.

"Fine, but I'm not talking to her," Nolan relented.

Cameron and I smiled victoriously.

We arrived back at Nolan's apartment just after two in the morning. Cameron and Jaime elected to sleep on the couch instead of driving home. Meanwhile, Nolan and I retired to his bed, where we quickly fell asleep.

***

The following morning, we drove downtown and ate at Meridion cafe, then returned to the car to retrieve the mirror from the trunk.

As we made our way to Lady Perida's shop, Cameron carried the mirror under a sheet that we'd borrowed from Nolan's bed to ensure that no one in town would recognize it.

Nolan held the door for the three of us, determined to hide at the back of our small group. I glanced at the floor, disappointed that he was so unwilling to form a relationship with his aunt. I'd give anything to have a living family member to lean on and I wished he understood.

Bells chimed against the glass as the shop door fell shut behind us. We walked past an arrangement of herbs and paused at the counter to wait for the psychic to appear.

"Hello, again," a muffled voice called from behind the tapestry.

Moments later, the familiar purple cane emerged from the back room, a wrinkled hand gripping its handle. The tapestry pulled back and Lady Perida stepped out from behind it.

"You've brought it with you, I presume?" Lady Perida asked.

Even after experiencing it a few times now, it was still difficult to believe she was legitimately psychic.

Cameron pulled the sheet off the mirror and carelessly attempted to pass it to Nolan, who dropped it. Rolling his eyes, Nolan leaned to the ground to retrieve the fallen sheet and held it up. He grimaced at the dust covering his obsidian sheets and unsuccessfully tried to brush it away. Giving up, he wadded the sheet in his arms and hugged it to his chest.

Cameron set the mirror face up on the counter. She adjusted her weight to lean on her cane and reached for the mirror with her free hand, brushing her index finger over a crack in the glass.

"I'm afraid I can't be of much help," Lady Perida spoke, her gaze not leaving the mirror.

Nolan snorted behind us and I closed my eyes as I let out a defeated breath.

Lifting her chin, she eyed Nolan.

"I can assure you, I would help you repair the mirror if I could," she spoke to him.

"You'll need to talk to Iliza Fadra at the glass shop down the street," Lady Perida explained. "Tell her it's a Victorian piece, and you'd like it to stay that way. Make sure you tell her I sent you."

"But, that's Ellie's mom. Won't she recognize the mirror?" Cameron asked, concerned about the prospect of being caught with the stolen mirror.

"We can tell her I broke it by accident when I was there that night. I'll tell her I took it to get repaired, rather than just leave it there," Jaime offered.

Cameron and I exchanged glances and shrugged. It seemed like a good enough plan.

Nolan looked like he wanted to say something, but stubbornly refused to acknowledge the psychic.

"So," I started, "I guess we should go to the glass shop."

"Cameron took the sheet from Nolan and wrapped it around the mirror as he picked it up from the counter.

"Thanks, Lady Perida," he said as he turned toward the exit.

Nolan let out a long sigh and looked at Lady Perida.

"Won't replacing the glass get rid of the mirror's capabilities?" he asked.

She smiled that he had spoken to her. "The glass was infused with lilac oil, a common ingredient used to communicate with spirits," she explained.

"That might have been important information to share," Nolan snarkily replied.

"Iliza will know what to do," Lady Perida assured him.

Nolan didn't seem to believe her, or maybe he was trying to convince himself that he didn't. I placed my hand on his bicep, and spoke softly into his ear, "Let's go."

He reluctantly turned to follow Cameron and Jaime out of the shop. I left after him.

Cameron stopped in the middle of the sidewalk and spun around, nearly hitting Jaime with the mirror.

"Am I going the right way?" he asked.

Nolan and I laughed, and Jaime pulled out his phone to look up the address. He looked up from his phone.

"Does anyone know what the shop is called?" he asked.

We all shrugged.

"I'll run back in and ask Lady Perida," I offered.

I jogged to the shop and walked in. As the bells chimed on the door, Lady Perida spoke from behind the counter, "Susquehanna Glass."

"Thanks," I smirked as I took a step back onto the sidewalk.

As I approached my friends, I raised my voice in Jaime's direction, "Susquehanna Glass."

Jaime nodded and typed it into his phone.

"Got it," he said, "that way."

He pointed in the direction Cameron had been leading us.

Cameron smiled proudly. "I'm a natural navigator."

"Don't make me tell the story about the time you lost your car in the parking garage," Nolan teased.

Cameron scoffed, "that was a fluke."

"Sure it was," Nolan chuckled.

We turned a corner at the next intersection and walked along the sidewalk.

"There it is!" I exclaimed, pointing toward a worn blue sign that read "Susquehanna Glass" in cream letters.

Nolan held the small door open for Cameron, who carefully maneuvered through it with the mirror. We walked past window displays and China cabinets before coming to a white counter at the back of the shop.

A tall woman with frizzy, white, shoulder-length hair looked up at us from her chair. Her ruby-colored glasses hung around her neck from a chain of beads of the same color.

"How can I help you?" she asked.

"We're looking for Iliza Fadra," I replied.

Jaime pulled the sheet from the mirror and bundled it up in his arms.

"We need help fixing this mirror," Cameron explained.

She leaned forward to peer over the counter and Cameron held the mirror higher so she could see.

"Lady Perida sent us," I added.

"I'm Iliza," she replied, nodding slowly. "Set it on the counter, let's take a look," she said, gesturing toward the countertop.

Without taking her eyes off of the mirror, Iliza grabbed her glasses and rested them on her nose.

"How did this happen?" she asked, running her finger over the broken glass.

"Uhh," I hesitated.

"The ghost of Landon Meridion broke it," Cameron spewed.

The woman eyed him over the frame of her glasses. It was hard to tell whether she believed him. She returned her attention to the mirror.

"It'll need a full glass replacement," she stated. "I assume the bill should be sent to the historical society?"

We looked at Jaime, unsure how to respond.

He gulped.

"Umm, actually, if we could just keep this between us," he said.

"Umm, I actually..." he struggled to collect the right words. "I work for the asylum and I bumped into the mirror by accident. I'm a klutz, I know." He laughed nervously.

"I'll just pay for it. I don't want the society losing money because of me." He smiled, hoping she'd accept his explanation.

"You work for the asylum?" she replied skeptically.

He nodded, sucking in his upper lip.

"Ellie said the mirror that went missing was the one from Meridion Manor," she quizzed him.

"I was doing research there," he repeated the same lie he'd told Ellie.

She nodded. "I do remember her saying she'd been frightened by someone the other night," she replied.

"Yep, that would be me." Jaime forced a laugh.

She looked at the mirror and let out a breath.

"I'll tell you what," she said, "Perida is an old friend, so. I'll fix the mirror free of charge."

Jaime grinned and placed a hand on his chest.

"That's so sweet, thank you," he said.

"Come by Saturday afternoon," she replied. "I'll have it ready by then."

As we walked back to the municipal lot, Cameron smiled and asked, "So...how about we plan that date night?"

"I'm free Friday night," I said.

"Me too," Jaime replied.

Nolan shrugged. "Works for me."

***

Cameron and I met Nolan and Jaime in the parking lot outside the restaurant on Friday night.

"Where to?" I asked as we got into Cameron's car.

"How about that place down on Baker Street?" Nolan suggested.

"I love their margaritas!" I replied.

"Me too!" Jaime agreed, turning from the passenger seat to high-five me.

Cameron put the car in drive and stepped on the accelerator.

"Who wants to be my karaoke partner when Margaritaville comes on?" he asked, and we laughed.

When we entered the bar, I immediately noticed Carter's painfully familiar shoulder muscles tensing as he shot a pool ball across the table.

I grabbed Nolan's arm and hurried him to the bar, hoping Carter would be too preoccupied to notice us.

We sat at the bar and ordered four strawberry margaritas. Nolan handed the bartender his card and said, "put them all on this."

"Awe, thanks," Jaime cooed.

The bartender set four glasses on the bar top, and we picked them up. We clicked the glasses together and Cameron cheered, "to The Ghostions."

"Ghostions?" Nolan raised an eyebrow before taking a sip.

"Yeah," Cameron smiled. "That's what I decided to call us. Ghost plus Meridions, Ghostions."

I couldn't help but laugh.

"We're ghost hunters now," he explained, taking a sip of his drink. "Every good ghost hunting team needs an official name."

I shrugged and took a sip, then held up my glass. "Ghostions it is," I agreed.

Jaime and Nolan joined in, tapping their glasses against mine and Cameron's.

"Ghostions!" Nolan and Jaime cheered.

We each took a sip and as I lowered my cup, a strong arm rested over my shoulder. I turned to see who it was.

"Hey, Zoey. How've you been?" Carter smiled.

"Uhh, hi Carter," I replied, cautiously.

Nolan shot Carter a warning glare and Carter looked at him, then removed his arm from my shoulder and held his hand out to Nolan.

"Nolan, right?" he said.

Nolan didn't respond, instead he stared at him intently until he lowered his hand.

"Alright then. Nice seeing you, Zo," Carter said as he walked back to the pool table.

"Asshole," Cameron muttered.

"He said it, not me," Nolan scoffed while sipping his margarita.

"Who was that?" Jaime asked.

"My neighbor," I replied.

"Her douchebag neighbor," Cameron clarified.

"He's not that bad," I sighed.

"He's a dumb jock," Cameron said to Jaime.

Jaime nodded, "got it."

Just then, the DJ's microphone clicked on and he announced, "karaoke sign-ups are now open."

Cameron chugged the rest of his drink and slammed the empty glass on the counter.

"Be right back," he said before rushing to the sign-up sheet.

We laughed as Cameron pushed to the front of the line and scribbled his song choice on the clipboard.

He returned with a smile. "Who's ready for some Jimmy Buffett?" he asked.

Nolan sipped the last of his drink and stood. "I'll do it with you."

"Heck, yeah!" Cameron cheered.

"Is there room for three on the stage?" Jaime asked.

"Four?" I corrected him.

"For the first serenade tonight, we have Phil McKracken," the DJ announced.

"Really, dude?" Nolan laughed along with a slew of bar patrons as Cameron raised his hand.

"Get it," Cameron snickered, "Phil McKracken."

"Grow up," I said, motioning for him to approach the stage.

The three of us followed a grinning Cameron to the stage, and he bowed, blowing kisses to the cheering crowd.

The DJ handed him the microphone.

"Hilarious," he said, clearly not amused.

The music started and the four of us huddled around the microphone as we swayed and sang the song.

The song ended and Cameron asked, "Who's up for another margarita?"

"I'm in," I replied, and Jaime and Nolan nodded.

We ordered another round and moved to the dance floor to enjoy them.

"We should do this again," Jaime said over the music.

"I agree," I replied.

***

The following afternoon, we met downtown and returned to the glass shop. Iliza looked up from her computer and stood as we walked in.

She knelt down behind the counter and lifted the mirror, placing it on the countertop.

"How do we know if it works?" Jaime whispered.

"It will work," Iliza snapped.

Jaime bit his lip, seemingly wishing he hadn't asked.

"I'm sure Perida told you this already, but if I were you, I wouldn't go messing with the spirits in the Meridion Manor," she said sternly.

"Oh, we weren't..." I said.

She held up a manicured hand. "Save it. I'm not here to scold you, I couldn't care less what happens at that manor. Just consider it friendly advice."

We nodded, and Cameron picked up the mirror from the counter.

"Are you sure we can't pay you?" Nolan offered.

She shook her head. "Just tell Perida I said hi when you see her."

We nodded and returned to the car with the mirror, which we tucked carefully into the trunk. Then, we went to O'Connell's for dinner.

As darkness fell on the streets, we got in the car and drove to the asylum.

***

Jaime parked at the asylum in the same place as last time and we watched from the car as he ensured the building was empty.

When he waved us in, Cameron quickly grabbed the mirror from the trunk and we rushed to the atrium. We climbed the stairs and speed-walked down the hallway to Edith's room.

Cameron passed the mirror to Nolan and stood in front of it.

"Hi, Edith. We came back with the mirror," Cameron spoke to his reflection.

Soon after, Edith appeared. Her figure was clearer this time, as if she wanted us to get a good look at her. She had on a hospital gown and her hair was ratty, sticking up in the back as if she'd just woken up. The skin under her eyes was puffy and sagged. Dried blood was matted into the hair above her left ear.

"What happened to you?" Cameron couldn't resist asking.

She slowly turned to glare at him, and Jaime sighed loudly.

"Edith underwent a lobotomy during her time at the asylum," he explained.

"How was I supposed to know?" Cameron shrugged.

"Didn't you tell him while you were in the lobotomy room last time we were here?" I asked Jaime.

"They were too busy making out to talk," Nolan laughed.

"Can we get back to the task at hand?" Jaime snorted.

"How do we do this?" I asked Edith.

She looked at the mirror in Nolan's hands and instructed him, "turn the mirror toward me."

He adjusted the mirror so that the glass was facing her, and Edith stared into the mirror as if she was trying to gather the courage to say something.

Finally, she said, "honey crisp."

The four of us exchanged glances, perplexed.

"It's our code word," Edith explained.

Martha's face appeared in her mirror and we watched in amazement as she and Edith studied each other.

"My Martha," Edith said sweetly.

"Mother," Martha replied equally as sweet, "it has been so long."

"I know, my dear," Edith sounded pained.

Cameron opened his mouth to speak, but Edith beat him to it, "thank you for bringing her back to me."

I replied, "of course."

She turned back to Martha. "My dear, I think it's time I told you the truth," she said.

"What is it, mother?" Martha softly inquired.

"I fear you will have no choice but to hate me," she began.

"I could never," Martha assured her.

I wanted to reach out and hold Edith's hand as she spoke, but there was nothing to hold but a reflection.

Edith held back a whimper, then said, "I never told you."

"What is it mother?" Martha was growing impatient.

"Martha, dear, Landon is not your father," Edith said, "Reginald is your real father."

Martha gasped.

"Popcorn would be awesome right now," Cameron joked.

"Dude, shut up," Nolan hissed.

"What happened to him?" Martha begged for an answer.

Edith let out a ghastly cry and revealed, "I believe Landon is responsible for his death."

The four of us held our breaths as we waited for Martha's reaction.

Much like we had the first time we'd heard the truth, Martha appeared stunned.

"He told me that's what he was going to do," Edith began to frantically explain. "I couldn't support him, of course. How could I allow him to kill your father?"

"You!" Martha shouted, causing all of us to flinch.

"You cheated on father?" Martha sounded angry.

"Martha, please," Edith tried to calm her.

"How could you do such a thing?" Martha cried, "It really is no wonder he sent you away!"

"I did no such thing!" Edith scolded. "It was before we were married. Hate me for that if you want, but do not accuse me of such horrid acts!"

"Then, why did he send you away?" Martha asked through tears.

"He sent me here because I wanted a search party sent to find you and Reginald," Edith confirmed.

"Why didn't you tell me the truth?" Martha pleaded. "You know how I adored Uncle Reginald.

"You adored Landon. How could I take that from you?" Edith asked rhetorically.

"He wasn't my real father. What did it matter about him?" Martha asked.

"Martha, dear, you have to understand," Edith explained, "I had no choice."

Seeing them both pause, I informed Martha, "Landon visited us after you left the other night."

"I'm sorry to have brought you into this," she said. "I just, I needed to know what became of Uncle Reginald, and you were the only ones who paid attention to me."

"Oh, Martha, it's okay," I said as she began to weep.

"What do you mean?" Nolan asked.

"Night after night, I appeared in the mirror and they never acknowledged me," she cried. "The two of you were the only ones," she added, looking at Nolan and I.

"That's horrible," Cameron said solemnly.

"Why didn't you just tell me you wanted to talk to Martha?" Jaime asked Edith. "I would've helped you."

"I couldn't ask you to do that," she replied. "Besides, I thought she was happy in the manor until the mirror broke again."

"You knew that the mirror broke?" Nolan asked.

"I felt it," she replied, "I presumed that Landon had destroyed it."

"Why doesn't Landon want you guys talking to each other," I asked.

"It would be detrimental to his legacy," Edith replied.

"He's afraid the word will get out that Martha isn't his daughter and his reputation will be destroyed," I said, realizing Landon's true motivations.

"Precisely," Edith replied.

"Well, at least you're together now," I said with a supportive smile.

Then, I turned to address my friends and said, "maybe we can find a way to talk to Landon and get him to leave all of us alone."

"I think I'd like to move on to the afterlife," Martha commented, "I won't have to worry about him there."

"I'll go with you," Edith told her.

Martha turned to me and asked shyly, "Would you do one thing for me first?"

"Of course," I replied without hesitation.

"Would you take us to Uncle Reginald, I mean...my father?" she asked, then turned to Cameron. "You said you'd seen him."

The four of us looked at each other and shrugged. "Sure," we said in unison.

Chapter 20

We made our way back to Jaime's car, Martha's mirror tucked under my arm and Edith's under Cameron's.

"Do we really have to go back into the orchard?" Jaime whined.

"It's to help Martha," I reassured him.

"But, like," Jaime replied. "Can't we summon Reginald to the manor or something?"

"Ellie is never going to allow that," I reminded him.

"We could just sneak in again," Nolan pointed out.

I shot him a wicked grin. "Since when are you the daredevil?"

He shrugged and admitted, "it was kind of fun."

"No," Cameron stopped us. "Reginald's spirit is in the orchard, we have to go there."

Jaime sighed. "Why can't ghosts come out during the day?"

"They do, silly," Cameron laughed. "But my infrared camera works best at night."

"You know," I scolded him, "not every interaction has to be filmed."

"How else am I going to become famous?" Cameron smirked.

Jaime rolled his eyes as we set the mirrors in the trunk, carefully wrapping them in blankets.

"Off to the manor," Jaime grumbled, "I guess."

Cameron patted his shoulder. "I'll hold your hand, you'll be fine."

"Gee, thanks," Jaime replied sarcastically as we got in the car.

***

We arrived at the manor late that night, and Jaime reluctantly followed the three of us to the edge of the trees. Cameron carried one of the mirrors in both hands as Jaime tightly gripped his biceps, constantly looking left and right for movement.

Leaves rustled to our left and Jaime let out a yelp, before covering his mouth with his hand.

"It was a squirrel," Nolan said, unamused.

"I know," Jaime said, trying to act tough.

Cameron snickered, and I stepped in front of him with the second mirror leading the way. We trekked through the orchard, our path illuminated only by the glow of the moon peeking through the barren tree branches above us.

Nolan casually whistled to himself as we moved further from the manor, and I froze in fear.

"Don't whistle!" I snapped.

"Why not?" Nolan raised an eyebrow. "I was just enjoying the walk."

"You can't whistle out here," I whispered, looking around at the trees, "they'll hear us."

"You're going to scare Jaime," Cameron scolded me.

"I'm not trying to scare him," I replied.

"Who will hear us?" Nolan asked.

"The skin walkers," I whispered.

Nolan's breath caught, and he asked, "What does whistling have to do with skin walkers?"

"It attracts them," I explained.

Jaime's eyes bugged out of his head and he stopped in his tracks to look at Cameron. "Is that true?"

Cameron nodded, and Jaime clung to him. "Are they going to hurt us?"

"If we don't provoke them, they won't," I said, turning to scowl at Nolan, "so no more whistling."

"I've never heard of this," Nolan replied.

"How?" Cameron asked. "I thought you took a class on it."

"Well, obviously, I know about the lore of Appalachia," Nolan replied. "But I've never heard anything about whistling."

"It's a thing," Cameron assured him.

"Just don't whistle," I hissed.

"Fine," Nolan said, holding up his arms defensively, "no more whistling."

Wind whipped through the trees, creating a frightening whistle. Jaime screamed and lunged at Cameron, causing him to drop the mirror. It landed in a pile of dried leaves and Cameron and Jaime toppled to the ground beside it.

"Come here often?" Cameron winked at Jaime, who'd landed on top of him.

Our laughter was cut short by a faint voice whispering among the trees behind me.

"What was that?" I whispered in a panic, looking around at the sea of honey crisp trees.

I couldn't make out any figures among them, but the voice came again.

"Did it say Reginald?" Cameron asked as he rose to his feet, extending an arm to pull Jaime up from the ground.

Nolan jumped and let out a fearful grunt.

"What is it?" I asked.

"I heard it again," he said, right in my ear."

We stood with our backs to each other, scanning the trees for the person or thing that was speaking.

"Father," another, more familiar voice said, and I turned to Nolan, whose attention was held by something in the leaves.

"Did you say that?" I asked.

He shook his head, and I followed his gaze to the mirror, where Martha had appeared and was calling out for her uncle.

"Get the other mirror!" Cameron yelled, excitedly pointing his camera at the one Martha was calling out from.

I quickly held the other mirror up to face Martha, and Nolan stood beside me to watch as Edith appeared.

"Is he here?" Edith asked.

"I sense him," Martha replied.

A muffled voice sounded to my left, and I turned to Nolan to ask, "What was that?"

He looked down at his wrist, his face pale. I followed his gaze to the face of his watch.

A man with a square face appeared foggy in the glass, his slicked back dark hair glimmering and his eyes soft.

"Father," Martha said again.

"Reggie," Edith said.

"Edith, is it truly you?" the man on the watch asked.

"It is!" Edith exclaimed, seeming as if she would cry tears of joy.

Nolan turned his watch face so that Edith could see Reginald.

"Oh, how I long to hold you Eddie," Reginald said.

"And I you," she replied.

Cameron cleared his throat and we all turned to him.

"Don't you have something to tell him, Edith?" Cameron said.

Reginald looked perplexed.

She sighed and hung her head, ashamed to face Reginald.

"I've told Martha" she said, "I fear Landon will come for us if we don't leave now."

Silence overtook the orchard as Reginald pondered her words. His expression was soft as he turned to Martha.

"Is it true?" he asked, "Can I finally address my daughter?"

Martha nodded, happiness evident in her eyes.

"How long has it been since you've told her?" he asked Edith.

Cameron, unable to contain his excitement, replied for her, "she found out yesterday."

"Martha asked us to bring the mirror here, so she could talk to you," I added.

Reginald turned to Martha.

"Loretta always said you looked like me," he said, adding, "I always longed to tell her why."

"There's something else," I said, and the spirits all turned to me.

I pointed to Nolan and said to Reginald, "he's your great-great-grandson."

"You're a Meridion?" Martha asked Nolan, a gleam in her eyes.

"A Bauer," Nolan corrected her, eliciting a prideful smile from Reginald.

"If you were murdered and buried, how did Nolan get your watch?" Cameron asked Reginald.

"I don't think it's polite to tell someone they were murdered," I scolded Cameron.

"Why not? It's true," Cameron replied.

"Because," I started.

"Not to worry," Reginald interrupted. "Landon and I had a bit of a scuffle one night in the orchard, and I haven't seen the watch since."

He met eyes with Cameron and added, "at least, not until you came to the orchard."

"I believe the watch was found by the historical society's groundskeepers," Jaime informed us. "They must have returned it to the Bauer family."

"It was my dad's," Nolan said, "so they must have given it to him."

Edith chimed in, "it was I who found the watch. I suspected Landon had killed him that night, so I used it to contact Reginald."

"How did the Bauer's get it then?" I asked.

"I instructed Perida to protect it when they took me away to the asylum," she explained.

I nodded, as did Nolan. Everything was starting to make sense.

"How did you know that Cameron had the watch that night?" I asked Reginald.

"I couldn't say for sure," Reginald replied, "it was almost as if I was being drawn to it."

"Like a trigger object!" Cameron exclaimed.

When the three of us didn't react, he clarified, "Martha and Edith are connected to their mirrors, and Reginald is connected to his watch."

The spirits nodded as if they understood what Cameron was saying.

I thought for a moment. Something still wasn't adding up.

"Then what is Landon drawn to?" I wondered.

"It must be something in Nolan's apartment," Cameron said.

"Why would it be something in my apartment?" Nolan asked.

"Because that's the only place we've seen him," I replied.

I thought for a moment, trying to think of anything I'd seen in Nolan's apartment that could serve as a clue.

"Doesn't your apartment have a historical marker on the front of the building?" I asked.

Nolan nodded.

"Sounds like we need to pay a visit to Ellie and find out about the history of your apartment building," Cameron said.

"I've got a better idea," Nolan stated.

We stayed silent in anticipation of his idea.

"There's a history book in my apartment about the historical buildings in the area," Nolan explained, "we should start there."

I turned to the spirits. "What are you guys going to do now?"

Martha smiled and replied, "we'll move on together. Thank you for your help."

"How do you move on?" Cameron wondered.

"We simply decide to," Martha replied.

"That sounds too easy," I said.

Martha shrugged. "Why does it need to be hard?"

"So, I guess we won't be seeing you anymore," Nolan commented.

Reginald smiled at his grandson. "We'll see each other again someday," he said, adding, "hopefully a long time from now."

"Are you ready to go?" Edith addressed the others.

"Wait," I said, causing the three of them to look at me. I met Martha's eyes.

"Would you help us with something before you go?" I asked.

She seemed perplexed as she asked, "What could *I* possibly help *you* with?"

I explained the dilemma with Nolan's landlord, then asked, "Could you help us prove that we're telling the truth?"

"Certainly," she replied, then turned to her parents.

"We'll wait for you," they assured her.

***

The spirits disappeared from their respective trigger objects and we hiked back to the car, then made our way to Nolan's apartment building.

The mirror securely tucked under Cameron's shoulder, we confidently marched into the leasing office, where Mr. Stevens sat behind his computer.

Looking up from his monitor, he greeted us with a sinister smile.

"Back with more doctored footage?" he asked.

I glared at him and held up the mirror.

"Back with proof!" I replied.

"What's this?" he laughed.

"Martha?" I cockily summoned her.

Mr. Stephens' eyes grew wider as Martha's face masked his reflection. He opened his mouth, but no words came out.

"How do you do?" Martha said, causing Mr. Stephens to flinch in surprise.

"Believe me now?" Nolan asked.

"How are you doing that?" he nervously asked, tilting his head to inspect the mirror.

"Mr. Stephens, meet Martha Meridion," I stated with a smile.

"It really is a pleasure to meet you," Martha said to him.

Mr. Stephens didn't reply, he just watched the mirror as Martha smiled at him.

"Trouble speaking?" Nolan asked.

Mr. Stephens swallowed.

"I hear my father caused quite the ruckus here," Martha said, "I apologize for his outbursts."

"Your...your father?" Mr. Stephens choked out.

"Yes," Martha clarified, "he can have quite the temper I'm afraid."

Nolan studied Mr. Stephens, and spat, "Believe us now?"

His face contorted into a grimace, and he snatched the mirror from me. He studied the mirror front to back as if he was searching for something.

"You won't find anything," Cameron told him. "It's real."

"Victorian glass, infused with lilac," I explained, "spirits can communicate through it."

"Especially when it's a trigger object," Nolan added.

He eyed us skeptically and held the mirror in front of his face to confront Martha. "If you're really Martha Meridion, tell me, what color is the carpet in your room?"

"There are wood floors in my room," she replied.

Mr. Stephens stared at the mirror and slightly closed one eye as if he was trying to decide whether to believe her.

He forcefully shoved the mirror back into my arms and walked behind his desk. He dug through a stack of papers and handed one to Nolan, along with a pen.

"What's this?" Nolan asked.

"The lease renewal," he replied, "if I were you, I'd sign it before I change my mind."

Nolan took the pen and paper from him and quickly signed the bottom of the sheet, then handed it back to Mr. Stephens.

"Thank you, sir," Nolan said with a grin.

"Get out of my office," Mr. Stephens barked, and we obeyed.

As the door fell shut behind us, I held up the mirror and the four of us huddled in front of Martha.

"Thank you," I said to her.

"My pleasure," she replied.

We made our way to Nolan's apartment, and I held Martha's mirror in my hands, facing away from my body.

Cameron held Edith's and Nolan held up Reginald's watch. Jaime stood in between and summoned each of them.

"Thank you for everything," Martha said to all of us.

We smiled in response.

"Ready?" Martha asked her parents, and then nodded.

We watched as the three spirits disappeared all at once. A strange sense of relief fell over my body, like the air in the apartment had gotten lighter.

"Did you guys feel that?" I asked.

They all shook their heads, and Nolan asked. "What?"

"It was almost like I could feel them move on to the afterlife," I explained.

"Really?" Cameron said excitedly.

"Yeah," I replied, "and, now that I think about it," I paused. "I felt the same thing just before the police came to tell me that my mom had died."

The three of them gasped.

"I wonder if I felt her move on too," I said, mostly to myself.

"Maybe you're a psychic," Cameron suggested.

I laughed. "I doubt that."

"Where's that book you mentioned?" Jaime asked Nolan.

He yawned and said, "let's find the book tomorrow, I'm tired."

We all agreed and went home for the night.

Chapter 21

I awoke the next morning in my apartment. Now that Nolan and I had started dating, officially, the bed felt empty without him.

I reached for my phone on my nightstand and smiled at the text that had come through just a few minutes prior.

Nolan: Breakfast at Meridion?

Zoey: Sure!

Nolan: I'll pick you up in fifteen?

Zoey: Sounds good

I got out of bed and showered in record time. Then, I slipped on a pair of leggings and a light blue hoodie just in time for Nolan to knock at the door. I struggled to untuck the slightly oily hair I'd elected not to wash from my sweatshirt as I approached the door. I turned the knob and pulled the door open to reveal a smiling Nolan.

"Ready to go?" he asked.

I nodded and followed him to his car.

Nolan parked in the municipal lot downtown and we walked hand-in-hand to the cafe.

As we finished our meal, Nolan pulled a well-worn paperback book from his hoodie pouch and set it on the table.

"Is this the book?" I asked, and he nodded.

I lifted the book and read the title out loud, "Historical Meridion: A complete guide."

He watched as I flipped to the index and skimmed for anything relating to his building.

"Hopefully, there is something in there about Landon," Nolan commented.

"What's the name of your building again?" I asked.

"Lackawanna Properties," he replied.

"There's a map here," I said, setting the book between us. We both leaned forward for a better view and Nolan pointed to a road.

"Orchard Path is right here," he moved his finger along the page and stopped, "so my apartment is here."

I moved closer to the page and read the label on the building he was pointing at, "22."

"What does it say 22 is in the legend?" I asked him.

He directed his gaze to the side of the page and read "Town of Meridion Planning Department."

"So it's an old government building," I replied. "I wonder when they turned it into an apartment building."

"Mr. Stephen's mentioned once that he bought the place in 1983, so probably around then," he responded.

"That's around the same time Lady Perida investigated the manor," I replied.

Nolan groaned.

"She's really not that bad," I said.

"Uh huh," he snorted.

"C'mon, she's the only family you have, at least give her a chance," I begged him. "She might be able to tell us something that could explain why Landon contacted you."

"We know why," Nolan replied. "He wants to protect his precious family secret."

"But we don't know why he's attached to your apartment," I clarified.

"The planning department would have been responsible for the construction of the railroad," Nolan explained, "maybe that's how Landon's connected."

"And maybe Lady Perida knows more about it," I replied.

"Maybe Ellie knows," Nolan countered.

I let out a sigh of defeat.

"Fine, we'll ask Ellie," I said, "but if she doesn't know, we're asking your aunt."

"Fine, fair enough," Nolan agreed.

"We can revisit it on Monday," I suggested. "Let's enjoy the weekend."

"Cam mentioned karaoke again," Nolan replied.

"Of course he did," I laughed.

***

Nolan and I spent the day together exploring a nearby nature preserve, then returned to my apartment for a homemade meal.

Just as we finished eating, a knock came at the door.

"I thought Cam and Jaime were meeting us at the bar?" Nolan said.

"I thought so too," I shrugged, placing our dishes in the sink before going to open the door.

When I opened the door, Carter was standing in front of it with a bouquet of wildflowers, my favorite. He handed me the flowers, and I took them suspiciously.

"I came to apologize," he said.

Nolan appeared behind me in the doorway and protectively placed an arm across the small of my back.

"I'm just here to say sorry," Carter assured Nolan.

Nolan eyed him hesitantly and Carter explained, "look Zo, I'm sorry I acted like an ass," he said. "You deserve to be treated like a queen." He looked up at Nolan and added, "I'm glad you found someone that will do that."

I smiled at Carter and for the first time in a long time, I saw him as more than just some football player from high school.

"Thanks, Carter," I replied. I lifted the flowers to my face and smelled them. "Thanks for the flowers, too," I added.

He smiled in response. "Can you forgive me?" he asked, "I would like to still be friends, I mean, if you're okay with that?"

I nodded. "I forgive you."

To my surprise, Nolan removed his hand from my back and held it out to Carter, who shook it.

"We're going down to the bars tonight if you're interested," Nolan told him.

"That sounds fun," Carter replied, letting go of Nolan's hand. "I'll drive," he offered.

I smiled. "Meet on the porch at 8:30?"

"I'll be there," he replied.

***

We met Carter on the porch a few hours later and he drove us downtown.

Cameron eyed me as if to say, "What the hell is he doing here?"

I explained, "Carter apologized and offered to drive us downtown."

Cameron narrowed his eyes suspiciously, and Jaime stuck out his hand. "Hi, I'm Jaime, Cameron's boyfriend."

Carter nodded and took Jaime's hand. "Nice to meet you."

The five of us awkwardly stood for a moment and Carter finally broke the silence.

"How about a round of drinks, on me?" he asked, adding, "as an apology."

I shrugged. "I'll never turn down free drinks."

Cameron nodded in agreement, and the four of us followed Carter to the bar.

"What do you guys want?" Carter asked.

"What's the most expensive cocktail you have?" I heard Cameron whisper to the bartender.

"I guess I deserved that," Carter laughed.

"How about rum and coke?" I suggested.

The others nodded, and Carter turned to the bartender. "Five rum and cokes, please," he said, setting his credit card on the bar.

The bartender mixed the drinks and set five glasses in front of us. We each took one and clinked them together.

After taking a sip, Cameron turned to Carter and asked, "Ever heard a song called "Margaritaville"?"

I laughed as Cameron, Carter and Jaime proceeded to the DJ booth to request Cam's go-to karaoke song.

Nolan and I sat with our backs against the bar and watched as they eagerly awaited their turn.

"Hey," a sing-song voice said to my right.

I turned to find Hana Brodwik hanging her purse on a hook beneath the counter as she sat next to me.

"Hi," I replied, politely.

"How have you been?" she asked.

"Good," I replied not sure what else to say.

After a moment of silence, she offered, "I saw you at the Halloween party last year."

I tried to hide a grimace as memories of my horrid batgirl costume resurfaced. How had I let Hana Brodwik see me in another homemade costume?

When I didn't respond to her comment, she added, "I loved your costume."

It was impossible to prevent my expression from morphing into surprise.

"Really?" I asked.

"Yeah," she replied, "it was so authentic."

It seemed like she was being genuine. I smiled, before responding, "thanks."

"See, I told you, you did a good job making it," Nolan nudged me.

"Is this your boyfriend?" Hana asked, eagerly.

"Yeah," I replied, leaning back so she could see him. "This is Nolan. Nolan, this is Hana," I introduced them.

Nolan waved at her and asked, "How do you two know each other?"

"We went to high school together," I explained.

Cameron's favorite song began playing and Carter's voice came over the speakers. "This one goes out to our favorite couple, Nolan and Zoey," he said.

The two of us laughed and raised our glasses to acknowledge them as they began to sing.

"You and Carter are back to being friends?" Hana asked, pointing to Carter.

"Yeah," I replied, with a smile. "He lives next door to me."

"He's still pretty hot," she said, muffling a giggle with her hand.

"He's single," I informed her.

"You think I should talk to him?" she asked.

"Sure," I shrugged. "He's matured a lot. Maybe you guys could be good together now."

She nodded and smiled as she watched his performance.

"You know," she said, "I'm really sorry about high school. I was such a bitch back then."

I waved it off. "It's fine. We've all grown up, it's time to move on."

She smiled and lifted her drink to tap it against mine.

"To starting over?" she offered.

"To starting over," I agreed.

When the song ended, our friends greeted us at the bar, and Nolan clapped.

"Bravo," he said as Cameron bowed.

"I'll be signing autographs outside," Cameron joked.

"Hey, Carter," Hana said, as he picked up the drink the bartender had just poured for him.

"Hello," Carter said smoothly.

I turned back to my friends and not long after, Carter led Hana to the pool tables. He spent the rest of the night teaching her how to play.

At the end of the night, we returned to Carter's car, and I asked, "So, you and Hana?"

"Yeah, seems like it," Carter beamed. "I got her number. We're going to go to see the new horror movie that's in theatres."

"That's awesome," I replied.

Chapter 22

After Nolan got out of work the next day, Cameron and I met him in the parking lot of Meridion Manor.

"Jaime couldn't make it?" Nolan asked Cameron as he shut his car door.

"No, he has to work late tonight," Cameron replied.

"That sucks," I commented, before adding, "we should probably head inside before they close up. The manor closes at five."

They nodded, and we walked inside. We found Ellie in her office, typing at her keyboard.

"Hi, how are you guys?" She greeted us.

"Good," I replied, "we're looking for some information on a historic building in town."

"Oh," she perked up, "I love talking about historical architecture."

"What do you know about the Town of Meridion Planning Department?" I asked.

She looked surprised. "I haven't been asked about that in a long time," she said, adding, "actually, I don't think I've ever been asked about that."

We watched as she searched for something on her computer and muttered, "interesting."

We waited for her to continue, and Cameron grew impatient.

"What's interesting?" he asked her.

She looked up from her computer and said, "it looks like it was sold to Brian Stephens in the 80s and then it was converted into an apartment complex."

I nodded, and replied, "yeah we found that out. Do you know anything about the history of the building before it was an apartment complex?"

"It looks like the building has a pretty significant history," she replied. "It was used as a meeting spot for the planning committee that orchestrated the construction of the railroad."

I nodded and looked at Nolan. "So that means it probably has ties to the Meridion family?"

"Oh, certainly," Ellie said. "Arthur was instrumental in the planning of the railroad. He likely would have been on the committee."

"What about Landon?" Nolan asked.

"Let's see," she said cheerily, typing into her keyboard. The typing stopped, and she nodded to herself as she scrolled.

"It looks like Landon took over as a member of the committee when Arthur passed away," Ellie explained.

"So, he probably spent a lot of time there?" I confirmed.

"I would say so," she agreed.

"Are there any mirrors in there, like Martha's?" Cameron asked, and I stepped on his toe as a way of scolding him for mentioning the stolen object.

"What?" he whispered.

"Not that I'm aware of," Ellie replied. "Strange thing though, Martha's mirror actually disappeared from the manor not long ago."

I eyed Cameron as if to say, "nice going."

Cameron faked a laugh. "Yeah, about that," he said, "we may have borrowed it."

Ellie raised an eyebrow, and I said, "I'm really sorry. We needed it for a research project, we should have asked."

"Where is the mirror now?" she inquired.

"In my trunk," Cameron replied, "I'll go get it."

Before Ellie could respond, Cameron bolted from the room to retrieve the mirror.

"What kind of research were you doing with the mirror?" Ellie asked, and I was somewhat amazed that she didn't seem the least bit upset.

I looked at Nolan and he quickly explained, "we've been talking to Lady Perida and she said the mirror possessed the ability to communicate with spirits."

"Yeah," I agreed, "and we know that the manor doesn't like paranormal investigations, so we took it outside the manor."

Ellie nodded skeptically.

"Why didn't you just ask? I would've loaned it to you," she said.

"My mom always said it's better to ask for forgiveness," I replied with a guilty smile.

Ellie burst out laughing. "My mom says the same thing!" she replied.

"Really?" I asked, just as Cameron returned with the mirror.

Ellie took the mirror from Cameron and inspected it.

"No damage, no problem," she said. Then she winked and added, "the board will never know."

"Thank you," I sighed, relieved.

She looked closer at the mirror and I was nervous she'd discovered something was amiss.

"The glass is so sparkly," she said, "you must have cleaned it."

I looked at Cameron and struggled to hold back a laugh.

"You could say that," Nolan replied, and Ellie raised an eyebrow at him.

"Trust me, it's better if you don't know," I said.

"While we're on the subject, though," Cameron said, "Do you know if there was ever a similar one at the planning building?"

She shook her head and replied, "as far as I know, this mirror, and the one at the asylum, are the only ones associated with the Meridions."

I thought for a moment. Then there must be something else in the building that Landon can communicate through. I wondered what else would be made from lilac infused glass.

"Ellie, when a building has historical significance, what aspects need to be preserved?" I asked, a hint of excitement in my voice.

"Anything used to build it," she replied, "the historical society strives to use era-appropriate materials.

She began listing them off, "doors, beams, siding, windows."

"Windows!" I exclaimed, "that's it!"

She looked at me quizzically and I quickly came up with an excuse for my elation. "We were rearranging furniture in the apartment," I claimed, exaggerating the look of guilt on my face. "Clumsy me, knocked the lamp right into the window and scratched it."

She nodded. "So the real reason you came here was to see if my mom would know where to find a replacement?" she asked.

"Exactly," Nolan replied.

Ellie laughed. "She keeps a small stash of Victorian glass, I'm sure she can help."

"That's great news," I replied, pretending to be relieved.

"I was starting to think I'd have to explain it to Mr. Stephen's," Nolan added, further selling our story.

"Ugh, he owns my building too," Ellie revealed with an eye roll.

"So you get it?" Nolan replied, and she nodded.

"We won't keep you," I said, "thank you so much for your help, as always."

"Anytime," Ellie replied.

We exited the manor and began walking toward the cars. As soon as we were far enough from the door Cameron said, "I can't believe she actually bought that."

"I know," I said, "I'm glad she did, though."

"We'll have to remember to thank Iliza for not telling her what happened to the mirror," Nolan added, and we agreed.

Leaning against Cameron's car, I said, "so, if the windows are made of Victorian glass, that must be how Landon is communicating."

Nolan nodded. "But how is he manifesting as a shadow figure in the middle of my room?" he asked, "Shouldn't he be appearing in the windows?"

"Maybe he's using the reflections from the window to make it look like he's manifesting in the middle of the room," I suggested.

"That would take a high level of intelligence," Cameron replied.

Nolan shrugged. "He was a successful businessman. Most businessmen are fairly intelligent."

I nodded in agreement.

"So, he's using the windows to his advantage to cast shadow figures, sure," Cameron said, "I can get behind that."

"But I still don't understand why the windows of the building would be his trigger object," Cameron added.

"Maybe we should ask him," I suggested.

"I don't have a better idea," Nolan replied.

***

Jaime met the three of us at Nolan's apartment for dinner and we waited for the moon to begin casting shadows into the living room.

"Which window?" Jaime asked.

Nolan pointed to the window at the front of the apartment.

"It's got to be this one," Nolan said, "it's the only window in the living room."

"But, he appeared in your room too," I pointed out, "maybe it's that window."

"Could it be both windows?" Cameron asked.

"How about two of us stand in front of this window, and two of us try the one in the bedroom? Then, just see which one he comes to," Jaime suggested.

The three of us nodded. It seemed like a reasonable enough plan.

Nolan and I stood in front of his bedroom window, facing the exterior of the apartment, and he pushed the curtains to the side. I grabbed his hand.

"Ready?" Cameron yelled from the living room, where he and Jaime were prepared.

"Yeah," I yelled back.

"On three?" Jaime said.

"One, two, three," Cameron said.

"Landon?" Jaime and I said in unison at our respective posts.

I breathed shakily as we stared at the window, but nothing changed.

"Anything?" Cameron yelled.

"No," replied.

Then a knock sounded from the wall behind us. We snapped our heads around to look in the direction of the sound.

There he was.

"Guys," Nolan hesitantly said.

"What?" Cameron asked.

"In here," I said, facing the figure across the room.

Cameron and Jaime appeared in the doorway of the room as Nolan and I stared at the shadow.

Cameron whipped his phone from his pocket and opened the camera app, determined to catch the mysterious figure on film. His phone screen went black and Cameron looked at the figure in horror.

"Did you drain my battery?" Cameron asked.

Lights flickered above and bulbs popped one by one throughout the apartment, shattering glass to the floor.

We stood speechless as the shadow morphed before our eyes into a man in a dark paisley vest and dress pants.

"Landon?" Nolan choked out, wrapping an arm around me.

I took a deep breath as I settled against Nolan's chest.

Landon nodded, appearing to casually lean against the wall.

"How are you doing this?" Cameron asked. "Why can you manifest and the others can't?"

Landon only laughed, seemingly amused by Cameron's questions.

"What is your connection to this place?" I asked.

He moved forward, towering above even Nolan, who stood over six feet tall.

"Do you have any idea how much time I spent here?" he barked, "How much hard work it took to build my empire?"

He stood straight and looked at Nolan. "I warned you not to meddle," he said.

"Are you upset that they turned this place into an apartment building?" I asked.

Landon chuckled, the black buttons on his vest bouncing up and down.

"What do I care about some building? It's only useful to me because of the glass."

"You're using the windows to manifest?" Cameron confirmed. "Why here? Why not at the manor?"

Landon smiled at him.

"The manor has a mere twelve windows on its best side," he replied, gesturing to the empty space around us.

"But here, here there are hundreds," he said.

"You're using this place for power," Jaime stated.

Landon's sinister smile grew.

"If you don't want us out of the building, what do you want, then?" I asked.

"I've told you already, have I not," he replied, turning to me.

"Stay away from my family," he barked.

"If we agree to stay away, will you leave?" Nolan asked confidently.

"It's a bit late for that. Don't you think so?" Landon replied.

"Please, just leave us alone," I begged, "we don't want any trouble."

Landon turned to me. "You know too much, dear. I'm afraid I can't do that."

"We won't tell anyone," Cameron assured him.

"Not a soul," Jaime agreed. Nolan and I nodded.

The spirit let out a guttural laugh.

"I mean it," I said, "no one has known all these years, nothing will change if we keep it a secret."

He smiled once more.

"You know," he said, pacing the room in front of us. "I happen to be a gambling man."

"What the heck does that have to do with anything?" Cameron snorted.

"Would you shut up, for once?" Nolan hissed, nudging him.

Landon's eyes peered into mine.

"Tell you what, dear. Swear on," he paused and turned to Nolan, then continued, "his life. Then, I'll leave."

I gulped and turned to Nolan. I knew at that moment that I would never do anything to harm him. Choosing my words carefully, I replied. "I'll swear on Nolan's life, *I* will never share your family's secrets."

Breathing heavily, we anxiously awaited his response. It almost seemed like he was teasing us with how long it took.

"Very well," he announced.

And with that, a sense of calm fell over my body and I knew.

"He's gone," I whispered.

We stood in silence for a moment, taking in everything that had happened. Then Nolan turned to Jaime, who was standing confidently to the right of the group.

"Look at you, you didn't cling to anyone," he complimented him.

Jaime smiled shyly and Cameron said, "we've been working on his confidence."

"It shows," I said.

Epilogue

Six months later

"**B**abe, where is my digital recorder?" Cameron shouted, his voice echoing from the trunk of his sedan.

Jaime stomped down the steps in front of Lady Perida's house, the device in hand.

"Right here, sweetheart," he said, handing it to Cameron.

Cameron tucked it into a pouch on his new equipment bag and laid the bag on the floor of the trunk.

Slamming the trunk shut, he smiled. "That's everything."

Nolan and I stepped onto the landing, Lady Perida at our heels. Her cane clicked against the floor as she steadied herself in the doorway.

"Let me know when you get there safely," she said.

"We will, Aunt Luisa," Nolan replied with a smile.

"Ready to go hunt some ghosts?" Cameron asked, a gleam in his eye.

"Toby the clown, here we come," I said, taking Nolan's hand.

We walked to the car and waved to Lady Perida as Cameron put the car in drive.

"Next stop, Ohio," Jaime announced as we pulled away from the curb and set off on a journey to capture Cameron's childhood ghost on camera.

Acknowledgements

Thank you to my husband, Roland for being supportive and for helping me with story development and editing.

Thank you to Grammy for always supporting my love for the paranormal. I miss watching episode premieres with you.

Also, thank you to everyone who has supported my writing career so far. Putting out my first novel was a daunting task. It was mostly written as a self-healing book with many nods to my real life. Martha's Mirror, on the other hand, is completely fictional which was a new, fun and exciting writing experience for me. I loved watching Zoey, Nolan, Cameron and Jaime come to life and at times even shape their own story. I am so excited to share the rest of *The Ghostions* trilogy with you in the coming years. Follow me (@author.jesswimmer) on Instagram and TikTok to stay up to date on my upcoming releases.

About the author

J ess Wimmer grew up in Flint, Michigan, but now calls Long Island home. She studied public relations and advertising at West Virginia University, where she honed her skills in storytelling and communication – tools she would later use to craft immersive worlds and compelling narratives.

A lifelong writer, Jess has been creating stories since fifth grade when she wrote a short historical fiction story for an English class. In 2025, she released her debut novel, *Fate Breaker: Return of the Queen*, a captivating blend of fantasy and romance that explores fate, power, and self-discovery.

Jess is always seeking new adventures, whether through the pages of a book or in the world beyond. Martha's Mirror is the second novel she's released, and the first novel of her paranormal/Victorian romance trilogy, *The Ghostions*. For information on book two of *The Meridions* and other upcoming releases, follow Jess on Instagram or TikTok, @author.jesswimmer.